PROTECTED HEARTS

BONNIE K. WINN

Steeple
Hill®

Published by Steeple Hill Books™

STEEPLE HILL BOOKS

Steeple Hill®

ISBN 0-373-81213-2

PROTECTED HEARTS

Copyright © 2005 by Bonnie K. Winn

All rights reserved. Except for use in any review, the reproduction
or utilization of this work in whole or in part in any form by any
electronic, mechanical or other means, now known or hereafter
invented, including xerography, photocopying and recording, or in
any information storage or retrieval system, is forbidden without
the written permission of the editorial office, Steeple Hill Books,
233 Broadway, New York, NY 10279 U.S.A.

All characters in this book have no existence outside the imagination of
the author and have no relation whatsoever to anyone bearing the same
name or names. They are not even distantly inspired by any individual
known or unknown to the author, and all incidents are pure invention.

This edition published by arrangement with Steeple Hill Books.

® and TM are trademarks of Steeple Hill Books, used under license.
Trademarks indicated with ® are registered in the United States Patent
and Trademark Office, the Canadian Trade Marks Office and in other
countries.

www.SteepleHill.com

Printed in U.S.A.

The night was dark and Emma shivered despite the warmth of the evening.

Sundance was nowhere in sight. Emma glanced next door at the empty house. No telling what the attraction was, but the dog was always lured by places he shouldn't explore.

Hearing a scratching noise from the far side of the vacant house, she ventured toward the sound.

But as she walked deeper into the yard, it seemed to get darker, the tall trees blotting out any trace of moonlight. Telling herself not to be silly, she rounded the corner.

Then stopped suddenly.

Lights flicked in the supposedly vacant home. And not normal lights. This looked more like candlelight, shimmering and uneven. Emma swallowed an unexpected taste of fear. *Where was Sundance?*

Twigs cracked as she shifted her feet, making her jerk around. Her heart pounding, Emma told herself to get a grip. There was no point coming unglued over nothing.

Turning back around, she slammed into something hard, something warm, something alive. The scream in her throat emerged as something between a shriek and a croak.

"It's you!" Seth McAllister spoke in disbelief.

BONNIE K. WINN

is a hopeless romantic who's written incessantly since the third grade. So it seemed only natural that she turn to romance writing. A seasoned author of historical and contemporary romance, her bestselling books have won numerous awards. *Affaire de Coeur* chose her as one of the Top Ten Romance Writers in America.

Bonnie loves writing contemporary romance because she can set her stories in the modern cities close to her heart and explore the endlessly fascinating strengths of today's woman.

My Beloved spake, and said unto me, Rise up, my love, my fair one, and come away. For, lo, the winter is past, the rain is over and gone.

—*Song of Solomon* 2:10–11

For Marita. What would I have done without you after moving to this alien planet? You are friend, family, cohort in criminally delicious humor. I miss you, Montana girl.

Prologue

Los Angeles

Rage made the wait tolerable. As Randy watched, assistant district attorney Emily Perry finally arrived home. But the long summer day still held too much light. He needed the cover of darkness.

He'd warned her. His brother was only eighteen—too young to spend the next decade in prison. But A.D.A. Perry hadn't let up, instead suggesting Kenny needed to be locked away. "For his own good."

What did she know about it? With her perfect job, house and family… Sure, Ken had pulled a job with a gun, but he was just a kid. Up till then nothing on his rap sheet was felony stuff. But Perry insisted it was only a matter of time before armed robbery escalated to murder. And she didn't care that Ken was too young to be housed with violent cons. She claimed it was the only way to turn his life around. Since Ken was too old to be sent to juvenile, she said she would recommend the safest prison possible. As though Ken could be safe in any prison. But the D.A. wouldn't agree to probation, said Ken could be paroled in two years if he kept his nose clean. As long as D.A. Perry was around, his brother wouldn't stand a chance.

Minutes turned to hours as night set in. Finally, the lights went out in the windows at the front of the house. Only an hour more and then he could be sure. He checked the time every few minutes, the indigo glow of his watch dial the solitary light in the car. Finally he was sure.

Emily Perry left her neighbor's home by the back door, entering her own yard by the gate at the back that connected the two houses. She felt the lateness of the hour in the inky darkness and the fatigue that played between her shoulder blades.

Emily ran a hand through her short, dark hair. She'd stayed longer than she'd expected, but she didn't mind donating her time to the neighborhood alliance. As legal counsel, she saved them fees that could instead be used to improve the park-and-rec center.

She rounded the garage, then headed toward the back door, hoping Tom hadn't locked her out. She glanced at the kitchen window and paused, wondering at the brilliance of the light. It took a few moments for her senses to register the pungent, unexpected smell of smoke.

Tom! Rachel! If they were asleep...

Panicked, she ran. As she neared the house she felt the heat. Before she could reach the door, the bedroom windows exploded, spraying shards of glass. Flames belched out as the sudden supply of air fed the fire.

Screaming for Tom and Rachel, Emily grabbed the doorknob. She ignored the searing burn the hot metal pressed into her hand as she frantically tried to turn the knob. To her horror, it was locked. She spun around and raced toward the front of the house.

As Emily shouted, JoAnn and Paul Morris, her next-door neighbors, ran outside.

"Call 911!"

JoAnn rushed back inside to comply.

Another window blew, the small explosion booming in the quiet street. Heedless of the danger, Emily tried to get inside.

"Emily, no!" Paul grabbed her as she reached for the door.

"I have to get inside!" she screamed, adrenaline propelling her forward.

But Paul was stronger, holding her back.

"Rachel! Tom!" she screamed.

Acrid smoke poured from the windows, searing her lungs, stinging so badly tears poured from her eyes. Or maybe they were from crying, since sobs consumed her as rapidly as the fire that ripped through the house. And took those she loved.

Chapter One

Rosewood, Texas. Two years later.

Seth McAllister ambled down the quiet street of the very quiet town. Rosewood wasn't what he was used to, but it was what he wanted now.

Having traded in his architectural design firm for a return to his roots, he hoped to establish a remodeling business. The local hardware store should provide a good source of leads.

Spotting the store, he paused outside to glance in. As he did, a woman kneeling in the window display area whirled around. He caught a quick and vivid image of long, blond hair, an arresting face and a slim body.

An instant later her face was even with his. She was obviously startled. Her eyes, an incredible turquoise, widened and her mouth opened a fraction.

Seth pulled back, the contact too close, too immediate.

At the same time, the woman rocked on her heels, looking abashed.

Seth quickly stepped to the door and pushed it open. As he entered, the woman scrambled from the window ledge.

"I didn't mean to startle you," he explained.

She brushed her hands against her jeans. "I'm not usually so jumpy."

After an awkward moment, he smiled. "Maybe we can start over. I'm Seth McAllister and I'm looking for the manager."

"Oh," she replied, still looking flustered. "I'm Emma Duvere." She gestured half-heartedly toward the window. "I don't work here. I'm decorating. But you don't want to hear about that." She took a breath, before her words came spilling out again. "You said you're looking for the manager.

That's Luke and he's out right now. Could you come back later?"

Seth nodded.

"Or you could leave a message for him," she continued, looking for a paper and pencil in the maze of cartons surrounding her.

"No, thanks. I'll come back."

"Okay then." Mild curiosity kindled in her expression.

But he'd moved to Rosewood to avoid explanations. "Thanks." Seth left quickly, glancing at his watch. He had an appointment with the realtor at the house he'd rented. It was just as well. He didn't want to run into the window decorator again. He'd had enough of questions, concern and curiosity for one lifetime.

Emma stared after Seth's tall, athletic form as he exited. Rosewood's population was small, but she hadn't run into him before. She would have noticed his handsome face, his dark hair that looked slightly too long, as if he needed it cut.

Funny. His face so close to hers for those few seconds had been disturbing. She'd had the odd sensation of looking deep into his dark eyes. It had made her feel vulnerable, this soul-searching moment between two strangers.

"Who was that?" Cindy Mallory asked, bringing in a box of fabric.

"Seth McAllister," she replied, absently rubbing the weltlike scar on the palm of her right hand.

"Well, well. *Stranger* in town," Cindy said, smiling. "Tall, dark and definitely handsome."

Emma reached for the box in Cindy's arms. "Thanks for helping me today."

Cindy's eyes narrowed. "That wasn't even subtle."

Emma kept her gaze on the fabric. "What?"

"Let me put it this way. If you'd been driving and changed lanes the way you just changed the subject, you'd be one big car wreck."

Sighing, Emma dropped the fabric. "Sorry. It was just…"

"What?"

"Nothing." Emma couldn't explain the connection she had seemed to make with him. It wasn't something she could put into words. "He could be new to Rosewood."

"We'll have to alert the Welcome Wagon. If there's no *Mrs.* McAllister in the picture, every single woman in town will volunteer for the assignment."

Emma doubted he was attached. His eyes were filled with too much loneliness. "Hmm."

"You're being the enigmatic one now. Something I didn't notice about him?"

Emma turned to look at the window, her back to her friend. "No. Just remembering that it wasn't so long ago that I was a stranger here."

Cindy's tone softened. "But it's home now, isn't it?"

Emma nodded. She didn't like to dwell on the time two years earlier when she'd first arrived in Rosewood. She'd left her parents, family and friends behind with no certainty that she would ever see them again.

Cindy seemed to understand what Emma wasn't saying. "Have you decided on the fabric for the window?" She pointed to the only unopened carton. "That was the last box."

Gratefully, Emma latched on to the safe subject. "I think so. And, Cindy, I really do appreciate your help. The store's so busy lately it takes nearly all my time."

"You know I love the design aspect of creating window displays. Besides, what are friends for?"

Swallowing, Emma silently acknowledged that the friendships she'd forged in Rosewood had rescued her, in so many ways.

The warm fellowship of the Community Church had been a balm to her wounded spirit. Cindy and her friend Katherine Carlson had swept her into their lives. Inviting her into their homes and families, the women had forged a bond that eased the pain, that sometimes diverted the loneliness.

And when Emma had opened her costume store, both had dived in to help, involving other members of the church as well. Without them, Emma doubted she could have set up the shop. At least not so well and so quickly.

In tune with Emma's quiet mood, Cindy didn't ask any more questions. Instead they worked together, assembling the design. It didn't take long. In keeping with the simplicity of the small town, Emma didn't strive for anything sleek or elaborate. After about an hour, Cindy had to leave to pick up her children, but Emma didn't mind finishing the window on her own.

Pleased with the end result, she packed up, stopping at her shop to unload the boxes before she went home. The store, Try It On, had emerged after her relocation under the witness protection program. Although they had had no proof Randy Carter was responsible for the fire that had killed Tom and Rachel, the D.A. was convinced he was their arsonist—convinced enough to believe Emma wouldn't be safe from him.

Initially, Emma had balked at leaving so much of her life behind. Not her occupation, though. She had no heart to practice law anymore. It had cost her too much.

It was a strange thing, as though she'd somehow gone backward in time, erasing that part of her life as wife and mother, starting anew as Emma Duvere. Even her blond hair was new. And she was starting over alone. Alone and lonely.

Sighing, Emma collected the day's orders to take home. When she'd been younger she'd wavered between her desire to pursue a career in law and follow in her father's footsteps, or to give in to her creative ambitions. After the horror of Tom and Rachel's deaths, even her father hadn't protested when she'd decided to leave the law behind.

The pain of loss clutched her as though it had been two days ago instead of two years.

The shop was quiet, crowded with costumes, bolts of fabrics and accessories. She was outgrowing the small space that had seemed overly generous when she'd purchased it more than a year ago. But now, costumes and all it took to make them filled each bulging nook and cranny.

Her assistant, Tina, had locked up and gone home earlier. The costumes seemed lifeless. No rustle of crinoline or soft swish of silk. They were all tucked in for the night. As she should be. However, today, as every day, she procrastinated, not wanting to leave. This was the most difficult time, coming home at the end of the day, knowing only her pets waited there.

Once Emma left, it didn't take long to drive from the center of town to her small house. Numb when she first arrived in Rosewood, she hadn't cared where she lived. But once she accepted the fact that she was in Rosewood for the duration, she'd contacted the U.S. Marshal and made arrangements to find something more suitable than the apartment chosen for her. Although there were complexities because of her new identity, the Marshal had helped her through the maze.

Emma's home had many qualities of the larger Victorians that filled the town. Detailed gingerbread trim outlined the steep roofline. And the original windows, some of them stained glass, made the place bright and inviting. It was very different from the sleek contemporary home she'd shared with Tom. But she couldn't bear to duplicate her previous life. And she had always loved the history of older homes, the feeling of continuity from one generation of owners to the next.

Emma pulled in the driveway, glad to see the lights burning cheerfully in her front windows. She took the precaution of using timers so that they were on before she arrived home. Not that crime was a factor in Rosewood. But it was in her life.

As she pushed open the door, her dogs, Butch and Sundance, danced around her feet, tails wagging in furious delight. Butch, a black Scottish terrier, was a touch more reserved. But Sundance, her incorrigible West Highland White terrier, held no such constraints.

As was her habit, she quickly walked to the old-fashioned, country kitchen and opened the door to the backyard. Bouncing bodies of fur charged outside. Without fail her dogs cheered her, making her seem less alone.

After filling their dishes, she glanced into the fridge. She didn't keep much food on hand. Seemed a waste for just one person. But tonight she wasn't particularly in the mood for a frozen dinner for one.

Emma glanced at the small pile of mail.

Nothing there intrigued her, either. She went back to the door and called for the dogs.

Within a short time Butch trotted over to her, ready to be petted and adored. But Sundance didn't join them. After a few minutes she called him again. Nothing.

"Where's your buddy?" she asked Butch.

Sundance was always the one who lagged behind, always the one most apt to get into mischief. She'd had Butch first and when she'd acquired the second dog, Sundance had proved to be more of a challenge. Knowing he would willingly go farther afield than was wise, Emma walked outside, calling his name. Anxiety was never far from the surface, one of the scars she now carried.

The sky was dark and Emma shivered despite the warmth of the evening. Sundance was nowhere in sight. After scouring her own yard, Emma glanced next door at the empty house.

She called out softly, not wishing to disturb any neighbors. Hearing scratching from the other side of the vacant property, she ventured toward the sound.

But as she walked deeper into the yard,

it seemed to get darker, the tall trees blotting out any trace of moonlight. Telling herself not to be silly, she rounded the corner.

Then stopped suddenly.

Lights flickered in the supposedly vacant place. Like candlelight, shimmering and uneven. Emma swallowed an unexpected taste of fear. *Where was Sundance?*

Twigs cracked beneath her light footsteps, making her jerk around. Emma tried to control the ridiculous pounding of her heart. There was no point coming unglued over nothing.

Turning back, she slammed into something hard, something warm, something alive. The scream in her throat emerged as something between a shriek and a croak.

"It's you! The hardware-store window lady!" Seth McAllister stared at her in disbelief.

Swallowing her fear and trying to disguise her ragged breathing, Emma nodded. "What are you doing here?"

"A better question is what are *you* doing here?"

Emma's fear was giving way to annoyance. "Answer my question first."

"This is my yard, my house." His clipped tones revealed the man's equal annoyance.

"That can't be." Suspiciously, she backed up a fraction. "This house is vacant."

"It was until I rented it," he replied, clearly still annoyed.

"You?"

"Yes. Which brings me back to my question. What are *you* doing here?"

Not certain whether to believe him and at the same time embarrassed that he might be telling the truth, Emma stuttered. "Sun…Sundance, I was looking for him."

Despite the dark night, she read the skepticism in his face. "As in Butch and…?"

Oh, this was just too embarrassing to explain. She straightened her shoulders. "Sundance is my dog, a Westie, white, tons of long fur. He has a habit of roaming."

He glanced over at the open gate. "Maybe if you kept that closed—"

"I only opened it just now to look for Sundance." Irritated that she was having to explain herself, Emma took the offensive. "I don't want to sound rude, but how do I know you've rented this house? I saw you for the first time today and now you're lurking outside in the dark."

"Lurking?" A flash of white teeth showed his amusement. "Are you suggesting I followed *you?*"

She was grateful for the darkness as she felt her face flush. "If you rented this house, why is it lit by candlelight?"

"Because the broker screwed up. He was supposed to have all the utilities turned on. As you can see, he didn't."

Plausible, but experience had taught her that she couldn't take anything at face value.

"So, where is this alleged dog?" he asked.

Startled from her suspicions, Emma listened for Sundance. She heard a faint barking from the opposite side of the yard farthest from her home. "That sounds like him."

As she followed the barking, Seth followed her.

It sounded as though the yelping came

from underneath the house. Trying to keep one eye on the man while at the same time watching out for Sundance, she crept along until she heard a whimper. "Sundance?"

The whimper grew louder.

"Where is that coming from?" Seth asked, reaching into his jacket pocket. He withdrew a flashlight, turning the bright beam on the path.

The house was on blocks, but wood skirting covered the open area. Cringing, she knew Sundance could find the smallest spot to crawl through and apparently had done just that. "I'm guessing he's probably underneath the house."

Seth directed the light over the closed area. "I don't see how."

"Terriers are bred to go to ground—to get into impossibly tight spots, then rout out their quarry."

"Wasn't aware there was any *quarry* to be hunted."

"The house has been empty for a while. Probably field mice have found their way inside."

"Great," he muttered. "So, how do we get the dog out?"

"I'll look for the spot he managed to crawl through and try to open it a little. Can I use the flashlight?"

"No."

Fear crowded her throat and made her step back. The flashlight was more than adequate as a weapon. But she refused to let panic show in her voice. "What?"

He knelt down. Then, as she would have done, he crawled along the siding, poking for an opening. Was this chivalry? Or did he just want to get rid of her faster?

After several yards, Emma heard Sundance growl. He'd no doubt caught the man's scent. "Quiet, Sundance." The growl gave way to a bark, then silence.

"This must be it," Seth announced, pulling on a flap of board that was now firmly entrenched in the soil. As the dog had wriggled through, he'd cut off his escape when the board had been pushed against some hilled dirt. Seth lifted the board and Sundance burst free.

Standing on his back legs, the dog

pawed Emma's knees until she picked him up. "You rascal," she chided.

Satisfied that he was still at the center of her affection, Sundance yelped to be released.

"Does he do this sort of thing often?" Seth asked, dusting off his jeans.

Chagrined both by her dog's actions and her own suspicions, Emma tried to smile as she put Sundance down. "Animals can be a bit unpredictable." The words were scarcely out of her mouth when the dog latched on to the leg of Seth's pants, growling again.

"Sundance!" Now thoroughly embarrassed, Emma reached out to unfasten the dog's grip. "I'm really sorry."

The man's face was too shadowed to tell if he was amused or angry. "Looks like he needs to learn not to bite the hand that rescues him."

Probably, but she didn't appreciate the criticism. And the tartness of her feelings crept into her voice as she grabbed the dog again. "Thank you for retrieving Sundance." She wrenched out the rest. "And... I'm sorry he didn't seem grateful."

"It's all right. Now you just have to decide whether I really live here or not."
Turning, Seth left as quietly as he'd arrived.

And Emma's fear came snaking back.
Clutching her dog close, she ran. And
didn't look back.

Chapter Two

Seth couldn't stop thinking of Emma's face. It had been filled with fear as she had scurried back to her own house.

What were the chances that she'd live next door? Well, it *was* a small town. Smaller than he'd realized.

Back inside, the house seemed even emptier. Of course it *was* empty. He hadn't brought anything with him from the city other than his clothes. After the divorce, he'd walked away from the house he and Carla had furnished with such optimism and promise. Every room, every object contained a memory he couldn't bear to take with him. So he'd rented a furnished apartment. Things he had no connection with.

He intended to buy what he needed in Rosewood. But his needs were less these days, his life leaner. In truth, bleaker. But the truth wasn't an easy companion.

Glancing around the lackluster house, he wondered if he should have bought instead of renting. Then he'd have something to do with himself. But he had no interest in reworking a house for his own use. No matter what he did with it, the place wouldn't be a home. That was gone forever.

Seth considered his choices. Takeout from the local burger place, reading by flashlight or calling it a night. Without electricity, television wasn't an option. Venturing back into town held no appeal.

Glancing out the kitchen window, he saw all the lights ablaze in Emma's house. Nervous type. Maybe she was a small-town spinster, spooked by her own shadow. But when he'd looked into her eyes that afternoon, he hadn't gotten that impression. He'd seen something he recognized.

He shook his head. He didn't even know if she was single. She could be married or engaged.

As he opted for his sleeping bag and an early night, Emma's face flashed through his thoughts. He doubted she was married. She seemed far too alone.

The shop was nuts. Emma had agreed to make costumes for both the local community theater's adult production as well as their children's play. While thrilled with the business, she and Tina were crowding each other. And they were running out of space to store the costumes. Plus, the high school's production wasn't too far away.

Tina squeezed one more costume on the already tightly packed display rack. "Emma, face it. Either we get more space or we have to cut back on orders."

It was a decision Emma had been avoiding for some time. But things were coming to a head. "Which would you vote for?"

"You know me, boss. I like being busy."

Emma felt the same way. "But what if I expand and the business falls off?"

Tina reached for a piece of chalk, marking a hem. "Executive decision, not my bag. But I don't think that's going to happen."

"Maybe just a small expansion," Emma suggested, her tone as tentative as her words.

Tina rolled her eyes. "Isn't that an oxymoron?"

But change was difficult for Emma. Since her life had been twisted inside out, she clung to the familiar. "I suppose."

Tina scribbled on the tag that accompanied the order. "By fall carnival, we won't be able to turn around in here."

"Good point." Emma glanced around at the familiar but compact space. Cindy had been urging her to expand for months, confident that Try It On was only going to be more successful, especially since the community theater had acquired a wealthy benefactor.

Adam Benson, a well-known oil man who split his time between L.A. and Houston, had retired to the Hill Country. He had a passion for the arts and didn't see why moving away from a major center of culture meant he had to be deprived of good theater. He'd endowed the local community theater, donating enough to build a new playhouse. His generosity also enabled them to purchase first-rate costumes. She had enough work to keep her shop busy all year.

Emma frowned as she looked at the overflowing storage space. The community theater now staged six annual productions plus a Christmas play. That was a lot of costumes, which she was in charge of archiving. Where was she going to put them?

The bell over the door tinkled as it opened. The UPS delivery man wheeled in a dolly stacked with boxes. The cartons filled the last bit of empty floor space by the counter. She stifled a groan. Maybe she *could* add a room. Certainly she could get a few estimates, see if the cost was within reason.

Tina glanced at the latest delivery and then at Emma.

She had to get those estimates now, before the shop literally grew through the roof.

By the time they had sorted out the day's

orders and deliveries, it was growing late. It was dark when she drove home. Again, Emma saw candlelight flickering next door. But rather than instilling fear, this time it triggered guilt. Seth must be her new neighbor—no one burgled the same place two nights in a row. Which meant she hadn't been very neighborly. Especially since he appeared to still be without power.

She ought to make the effort, cook something for dinner, take it over.

Keeping to her routine, she put the dogs out back—after making certain the gate was firmly closed. Of course, if Sundance smelled something, he'd find a way out. She could have put them in the dog run, a chain-link enclosure with a roof, which they couldn't escape from. But she didn't like to limit them to the small space. She watched her dogs carefully, herding them back inside before Sundance could wander.

As soon as they were in the kitchen, she turned all the locks on the back door with a shiver of relief. Her resolve weakening, she opened the refrigerator. She could defrost some chicken. There were enough ingredients in her pantry to assemble some sort of dish to offer her new neighbor. But she thought of the flickering candlelight, the fear she'd felt the previous evening. Closing her eyes, she sank back against the counter.

And her resolve disappeared altogether.

Over the next week Seth distributed more of his business cards than he'd expected to. Still, he was surprised by the phone call from Michael Carlson, setting up today's meeting. Carlson owned the largest construction company in the region.

Sitting across the desk from him, Michael was gracious but forthright with his proposition. "I get a lot of calls from people who need work done, but the job's not big enough to dedicate a crew to it. I'd like to have someone reliable who I can refer. Luke over at the hardware store gave me a call, told me about you."

"In a small town like this I'm surprised you don't have a list of independent contractors."

"I do." Michael smiled ruefully. "I've

hired the best of them to head my crews. There are still plenty of one-man outfits, plumbers, painters, electricians. But not a general contractor I feel good about recommending."

"Then you're going to need some references."

"I'd like to see some of your work."

Seth nodded. "That's reasonable. Fact is I haven't done much contracting in several years."

"You're just getting back into it?"

"Getting back to my roots, so to speak. Remodeling paid my way through school."

"What did you study?"

"Architecture. Which is what I've been doing since I graduated." Seth braced himself, expecting Michael to grill him.

"That's a great asset for a contractor. Do you have some older jobs I can check out?"

Seth had prepared a list, which he handed to Michael. "The majority are in Dallas. But you'll find phone numbers there for contacts with several major construction firms."

"I have to say this is very impressive."

Michael lowered the paper and Seth could see the question in his eyes. Why was Seth going backward on his career path? "Perhaps I should be recruiting you to head one of my crews."

"I'd rather work on my own."

Michael met his gaze, his own measuring. "I can respect that. It was hard for me to learn to delegate—especially since I started this business by myself with only a tool belt."

Seth glanced around the luxurious office. "You've done well."

"I've been blessed," Michael replied simply. "I moved to Rosewood myself not that many years ago. I found the people to be welcoming, genuine. I hope you feel that way."

"I haven't been here all that long," Seth hedged.

"Took me a while, too." Michael glanced down at the paper. "I'll make a few calls and get back to you. When would you be ready to take referrals?"

"Any time."

"You're all settled in then?"

Seth thought of his near-empty house. "I'm getting there."

"Good. It doesn't take much to figure out things in Rosewood, but if you need a hand, call."

"You haven't checked my references yet."

"That's business. But when you're new in town sometimes you need a neighbor more than work."

Seth blinked. "That's a far cry from how things are done in Dallas."

Michael chuckled. "I guess so. Before Rosewood I lived in a different town, but it was just as small. So I guess it's second nature. Welcome." He extended his hand.

Accepting the handshake, Seth sensed Michael's sincerity. He was glad to have met this man. If he still believed in signs of good fortune, he would have thought this was one.

A week later, Emma still hadn't made a solitary neighborly gesture toward Seth McAllister. And that wasn't like her.

She hadn't made a decision about enlarging the shop, either. And the situation was past dire. Try It On had just been commissioned to make new choir robes.

Emma was delighted at the chance to update and redesign the robes—the Community Church had a wonderful choir. She was already sketching out ideas in her head. Which was a good thing since her draft board was now buried under the last delivery. She'd considered taking the drafting table home, but that would only complicate matters. The fabric and tools she needed were here at the shop.

Luckily, Cindy had again volunteered to help, this time to organize the overflow. She held up a bolt of fuzzy pink fabric. "Where do you want me to put this?"

The space where the fake fur had been was now filled with another bolt of material. "I swear they multiply at night after I leave." Emma rubbed her forehead. "For now, on the cutting table."

"That's already stacked a mile high."

Emma sighed. "When did everything get so out of control?"

"It's not so much out of control—it's that you're out of room. Face it, Emma, push has come to shove. Why don't you call Michael? He'll give you a fair bid and he won't run over budget with a bunch of *unexpected* costs."

Michael was a friend from church and Emma knew Cindy was right about him. He would be more than fair. "I wish I were more flexible, open to change—it would make this easier."

"We are who we are," Cindy replied.

"How did you become so wise?"

"I had plenty of practice doing dumb things. I guess after a while some of it had to sink in."

Emma finally smiled. Cindy was kind, generous, full of life and fun. But definitely not dumb. "Uh-huh."

"So, are you going to call Michael?"

"Yes." Emma took a deep breath. "You're right, it's past time. And I trust him completely. How could I go wrong?"

Emma was still coming up with disaster scenarios as she pulled into her driveway that evening. Having taken her courage in hand, she'd called Michael. And he'd recommended one person. Seth McAllister. Her mysterious next-door neighbor. The one she'd deliberately been unneighborly toward.

Surreptitiously, she studied his house as she collected her bag. Why in the world had she convinced herself that the man was a danger? Michael had nothing but high praise for Seth. And Emma had jumped to conclusions. It wasn't a move worthy of her belief system.

As she walked inside, Emma greeted her dogs absently. When they ran outside, she paused, looking at Seth's house. She thought of how lonely she'd been when she moved to Rosewood and instantly felt guilty. Well, it wasn't too late.

She could cook a pretty decent lasagna. And luckily, she had everything she needed. The previous evening she'd made a big vat of spaghetti sauce. Once the wavy lasagna noodles were cooked, it didn't take long to layer the casserole and then pop it in the oven.

As it baked, she took some time to freshen her makeup and change from her work clothes into a sleeveless yellow cotton shirt, cropped pants and sandals. She added a splash of cologne for courage, then traded her discreet pearl studs for cloisonné earrings that dangled just enough to frame her face. Satisfied, and refusing to primp one more second, she checked on the lasagna. It was ready. Taking a deep breath, she convinced herself that she was, too.

"Okay, boys," she addressed the dogs. "I'll be right back."

Cocking their black and white heads in identical positions, they watched her leave.

"Welcome, neighbor," she muttered to herself as she approached his house. "No, that sounds like I'm from Mayberry. Welcome to the neighborhood. That's better. Welcome to the neighborhood."

"Thanks."

Emma jerked her gaze from the benign sidewalk to the not-so-benign expression on Seth's face. "Um, hello."

"Hello."

She stared back at him.

He smiled. "Don't tell me you're at a loss for words."

She blushed with remembered embarrassment. Great. All she could do apparently was babble or stare. "No. Not at all. I've come to say welcome."

His eyebrows lifted so slightly she wondered if she imagined it.

"Again, thank you."

Emma waved the tips of her oven mitts. "This just came out of the oven. I hope you like lasagna."

"Yeah. I do. But I'm not sick."

"It's not chicken soup. And from experience, I know it's hard enough to unpack without having to cook."

"So you cooked for me?"

That assessment seemed too personal, so she lifted the lasagna. "Could we put this in your kitchen?"

"Sure." He started to reach for the dish.

She pulled it back a few inches. "It's too hot to handle without the mitts."

He turned and opened his kitchen door for her.

Emma's first impression was disappointment. The room was so bland, without any personality. But, of course, he hadn't had time to decorate. She put the casserole on the cool, empty range burners. "Looks like you haven't started dinner."

"No. I'm not into cooking."

Which meant he probably lived here alone. But she refused to give into the temptation to pry. "When I first moved here I lived on takeout. Some of the neighbors brought cookies, but even I can't live on sugar and chocolate alone."

He pointed to a counter piled with plates of cookies, brownies, pies and cakes. Maybe Cindy was right. The word must have gotten out to the single women of Rosewood: handsome, single man on Elm Street. Catch him while he's fresh.

But Emma didn't rise to the obvious. "I hope you have a gallon of milk to wash those down with."

He grimaced.

"Or coffee," she amended. Self-consciously, she gripped the oven mitts.

"That's one staple I'm never without. Would you like a cup?"

"I don't know, I—"

"You aren't going to leave me to polish off these delicacies by myself, are you?"

Emma didn't know how to flirt. She was so out of touch, she wasn't even certain that's what he was doing. But then it was coffee, not a date. "I guess I could have a cup," she conceded.

Again she thought she saw that barely visible motion with his brows. "Have you eaten dinner?"

"No. But having a cookie won't spoil my appetite."

He scrounged around the counter, finally coming up with two mugs. "Good. Then we can have the lasagna for dessert."

She flushed. "I don't mean to impose. I made the casserole for you…and, well, your family." She stood abruptly, poised to flee.

"No family," he replied shortly, shifting back into his earlier intense mood.

She was mortified. "I'm not trying to pry." Her words were stiff. "I'm a private person myself and I don't appreciate it when *well-meaning* people poke around in my personal affairs."

His gaze appraised her. "No harm. No foul. You'd have seen soon enough that I live here alone."

Because of their close proximity. Which meant he would know the same about her soon enough. "Me, too," she blurted. "Live alone, I mean. Except for my dogs."

"The hole-in-the-wall gang; I remember."

Her nervousness lessened a touch. "Yes. But they're not breaking and entering today. I left them in the house."

"They don't shred your place while you're gone?"

She smiled. "They have their moments, but for the most part they're well behaved."

He didn't argue the point. "I hope you don't mind paper plates."

"Not at all." There weren't any moving cartons in the kitchen. Either he'd already unpacked or there was little in the way of dinnerware to fill the cabinets. She wondered if he was recently single.

He put two mugs on the bar beside the disposable plates and plastic forks. Certainly no sense of cozy home and hearth. Her guilt multiplied. She should have made this visit earlier.

Climbing onto the bar stool he indicated, she realized at the last moment that Seth would be sitting close beside her rather than across the safe length of a table. Unaccustomed these past years to a male presence, she caught her breath when his arm brushed hers as he sat on the adjoining stool, then scooped out two generous portions of lasagna. He was tall…tall and powerfully built. Her nerves jumped to alert.

"I hope you like the lasagna…most people like my spaghetti sauce. I use lots of fresh vegetables and let it simmer for hours. And I make a really huge vat, enough so that I can freeze some in smaller containers. And, like this time, I make up some lasagna…I have to bring a casserole to a potluck Saturday night, so I'll use some of it then."

"Right."

"I'm sorry. Am I babbling? I babble when I'm… well, when I meet new people." *Men, she added to herself.* But none had affected her like this. No doubt it was how close he was. Both beside her now and living in the house next door.

"Don't apologize. At best I'm not much of a conversationalist. And I don't know anything about cooking."

"It's not usually my favorite subject, either." She poked her fork into the melted cheese on her lasagna. "Actually, there is something I'd like to talk to you about."

"Oh?" Wariness tinged his dark eyes.

"Yes. I own a costume and design shop in town, Try It On. That's the name of the shop, I mean. And I'm thinking of adding on to it. When I first bought the space it seemed more than adequate, but I'm outgrowing it."

"Business must be good."

"Yes, actually, it is. But we can barely turn around now. I've resisted the inevitable, but I think it's time I take the plunge." She met his curious eyes. "Which is what I wanted to talk to you about."

He studied her. "Why me?"

"Well, Michael Carlson recommended you."

"You know him?"

She nodded.

"This *is* a small town."

"Yes, but I've found that to be a good thing in most ways."

"Hmm. So tell me about this shop of yours."

Warming to her favorite subject, Emma described at length her business and the store's layout. "And my assistant, Tina, is certain we'll pull in even more business now that I've started designing storefront displays. You know, like the first time we met."

His gaze caught hers and she was sharply reminded of the encounter, that intense vulnerability she'd felt.

He glanced away, picking up his coffee. "When do you want a bid on the work?"

She blinked. "I hadn't decided."

"My schedule's open right now."

But it probably wouldn't be for long, she realized, with Michael's glowing recommendation. If she was going to do this, she needed to do more than wade at the shore. It was time to dive in. "Tomorrow then?"

He met her eyes again and she warmed under his intent gaze. "Tomorrow."

Chapter Three

Seth arrived early, well before opening. Emma Duvere was his only client. He didn't need the money, but he did need the work to keep himself busy, to keep his mind occupied with anything other than memories.

Emma was an odd bird. Quiet and thoughtful one moment. Nervous and distracted the next. He wondered if she was that antsy around all men or if he'd struck some agitated chord. Not that it mattered. She needed him for his work skills, not his social ones.

It didn't take her long to show him around the small shop. She hadn't exaggerated. The place was crammed to the limit. As he took measurements he understood why. There wasn't enough square footage, and the available space wasn't being used to its potential.

He double-checked the reading on his measuring tape. "Are the dressing rooms used frequently?"

Emma nodded. "All the time. Why?"

"They seem cramped, especially for some of the larger costumes."

"You're right—it's a problem. Still, I hate to give up more of the display area."

"You don't have to. If we moved the dressing rooms to one side, we could enlarge them and gain display space."

"That's a great idea! My displays seem to be shrinking daily."

"Would you like me to sketch out some plans? I think most of your space could be put to better use."

She looked at him doubtfully. "You mean change the entire shop?"

"Not in character, just layout. You need more storage—the obvious place to extend is out back. And if we add a delivery entrance to the new storeroom, it will improve the traffic flow."

"When the UPS man comes, we do have boxes stacked right in the middle of everything," she mused. "I knew the shop didn't have a rear entrance when I bought it, but I hadn't run a retail business before and I wasn't really thinking about deliveries."

"The building has character, which attracts customers. I wouldn't suggest changing that. We can keep the integrity of the building in the addition, do some faux aging and make it look as though it's always been here."

She cocked her head. "It sounds as though you're far more knowledgeable than a remodeling contractor."

"I've worked in design," he admitted.

She smiled, not a frantic gesture, but an easy smile that lifted her generous lips and softened her expression. "It's addictive, isn't it? Design, I mean."

"In many ways," he agreed. But not so much that he couldn't leave it behind.

Emma's smile faded. "This all sounds wonderful, but will it cost a fortune?"

"Give me a little time to work up the plans and I'll put some figures together. In the meantime, I'd like you to think about any other changes you've wanted to make. It's more cost-effective to include them at the beginning."

"You mean I'll have to figure out everything *now?*"

He smiled at the panic in that last word. "No. Plans can be flexible. But if I know going in, for example, that I'll be enlarging a doorway, I won't have to reframe it later."

"That makes sense. It just seems so daunting."

"If you let it be. Once you agree on a vision for the shop, much like the ones you come up with for your costumes, you simply plan it out and stick to the pattern."

"If you say so. But when I misjudge a measurement, I don't have to tear down a wall to correct it."

"I hope that won't happen. But it wouldn't be a disaster. I've put up walls I later decided I didn't want. And they come down a lot faster than they go up."

"Is that supposed to be reassuring?"

She looked so serious and so worried that he amended his brisk, business tone. "Yes. With a good plan, we won't encounter too many obstacles, and, if we do, they can be dealt with easily enough. Better?"

"Yes. I guess it is. I must sound terribly doubtful, but I've had difficulty with changes since I've moved to Rosewood."

Immediately he wondered why.

"And," she continued, "this is a big change for me. I like the cozy feel of my shop. It's been good for me. And I'm a little intimidated at the thought of it being so different."

"Larger doesn't mean impersonal."

Relief flickered in her clear turquoise eyes. "You're so certain?"

"Nothing in life is certain."

She swallowed and he realized his blunt honesty had touched a sensitive spot. "No, it's not."

"Do you still want the sketches and bid?"

"Yes…of course. I can't be a dinosaur in a space-shuttle world."

"All right, then. You know where to find me when you've had a chance to consider any other changes you want to make."

She smiled, but he sensed it was only out

of politeness. And he hated that he was wondering why. Emma was a neighbor, a possible client. That was all. He didn't need to know why there was a sadness in her big eyes when she thought no one was looking. And he didn't need to share his own private pain. He was done with that. Done with anything that could touch his heart.

Emma thanked him for his time and offered him coffee. But he told her he wanted to get started on the plans. And he did. But mainly he wanted to get away from her and the memories she'd accidentally prodded.

By the next evening, Emma's list had grown beyond her expectations. A special nook for her drafting table would make her job much easier. She could keep her designs separate from the stock and sewing areas. Now that she'd finally decided on the addition, she was growing excited.

She could expand her designs, produce an even greater diversity of costumes. Butch stood on his hind legs and nudged her knee with his nose, seeking attention.

"Am I ignoring you?" she asked, rubbing his ears.

His expression said he adored her regardless.

Still, she wandered into the kitchen, opening the jar of dog treats. Sundance had followed them and sat beside Butch wanting a goody, too. Emma obliged.

As she put the jar back on the counter she glanced outside. The lights were on next door at Seth's. She wondered if he'd begun her sketches. Emma picked up the list she'd been working on, itching to show it to him.

It wasn't late. Before she could change her mind Emma marched out the door. Keeping to the neighborly route, she knocked on his kitchen door.

After a few moments, Seth jerked open the door, startled to see her there.

That's when it occurred to her that she was being presumptuous. "I hope I'm not interrupting." Lamely she held up the paper. "You said you wanted a list of any changes I could think of."

"Right. Uh, come in."

Wishing she hadn't been so impulsive,

Emma entered gingerly. "You know, I could just give you the list, let you read it over."

"It would be better if we discuss it. Then I can be sure I understand what you want."

What she wanted right now was to have resisted the urge to dash over here. "Okay."

He led her through the kitchen to the living room. The only furnishings in the bare room were a large drafting table and a computer desk. He must have gone through a divorce. No one got to their thirties without collecting more than this. Unless it was all lost in a fire.

He pulled the chair from the desk, scooting it next to the drafting table. "Have a seat. I want you to see what I've drawn up so far."

As she did, he straddled the stool in front of the drafting table and once again she was seated within inches of him. Seth didn't seem to notice, however. The light on top of the board was already on and she realized he must have been working on the plans when she arrived.

She recognized her shop. True to his word, he'd kept the integrity of the architecture. Her gaze was drawn to other specifics, though. "You've moved the sales counter, too."

"It seems crowded now at the front door." Seth pointed to one side of the sketch. "I've opened that space for display area. Instead of only hanging costumes against the walls, you could run two rows where the counter is now. And moving the counter farther back will give you handier access to the new storeroom. You'll be able to check deliveries without leaving the sales counter."

She tilted her head, studying the sketch. "When I first opened the shop, I liked greeting customers as they came in, but it *has* gotten awkward as the space filled up."

"That and some customers would probably prefer to browse on their own when they first come inside. But you can still keep it personal. Add a few overstuffed chairs and side tables to the alcove. It would give your male customers a place to chill while their wives and girlfriends go through all the racks."

She smiled at him. "Purse-holders, I call them."

"Exactly. And they'll be more patient if you stock a few magazines that don't have dating quizzes, diets or anything called shabby chic."

Emma laughed, amused by his accurate description. "*Fish & Stream* be all right?"

"Yep."

"I definitely like the idea of the sitting area."

"I wouldn't be surprised if we find a fireplace walled up in the shop, as well."

"Really?"

"The age of the building tells me it should have a fireplace. The furnace is a later addition."

"A fireplace could be a great focal point," she mused.

"What would you think of enlarging the front windows?"

She looked at him with wonder. "That was on my list. Now that I'm doing window design as well, my own displays should be an advertisement."

"I was thinking bay windows."

Ooh. Emma loved bay windows. "I can see the curve of the glass, almost like a Victorian curio cabinet! Is that what you mean?"

Surprise lit his eyes. "That's exactly what I meant."

Emma warmed beneath his appraising gaze. "I told you. I get all caught up in design."

"So what else is on this list of yours?"

She explained the nook she envisioned for her drafting table.

"That should be situated somewhere quiet. What if it's part of your office?"

"But I don't have an office."

Seth pulled out a second sketch. "The attic isn't being used for much more than your furnace and duct work. It's a waste. But I can't see it being used for display or dressing area. It's a half story higher than your main level. If we close off the furnace room, we could open up the other part, section off an office/design area for you and a second smaller office."

"A *second* office? I don't even have *one* now!"

"You're extending your business, which means more receipts, more records. If you plan ahead, you won't be crowding yourself into one office, especially if you end up hiring more help."

She was quiet, reflecting on his suggestions. "Actually, you've given it more thought than I have."

"I've designed enlargements for a lot of growing companies. The hardest part for the business owner is to visualize just how much expansion is needed. Most underestimate it. Then you're looking at another expansion, which doubles the cost. My mother had an expression for it: pennywise, pound-foolish."

"I can see that." She lifted her gaze. "I'm fortunate to have found you."

He didn't move a muscle.

"To remodel the shop," she added quickly. "You clearly know what you're doing."

"I've had a lot of experience. A good designer gives you options." He pulled out a third sheet of drawing paper. "Here's another way to go at it—adding only the storeroom you requested, along with moving the dressing rooms. We can add or take away any of these elements."

The options were overwhelming. Emma glanced from the scaled-down version to the one she instinctively knew would work best. "I like your original. When you have an estimate, I'll talk to the bank, make sure they'll finance the addition."

He nodded, then withdrew a materials list. "I assume you want to use good materials, but you don't want to pay for a Jag when a Chevy will do."

"You read my mind. If the price gets too high, I won't be able to expand."

Seth pushed back a bit on his stool. "Have you considered buying or leasing another property? A building that's already large enough?"

"I don't want to move. I have a good location—which is the reason I chose it. Why? Are you having second thoughts about the job?"

"No. But you ought to consider every option, whether it means a job for me or not. I'll firm up the figures. I should have them by tomorrow."

Emma felt herself deflate. "Wow."

"Some people agonize over choosing a design for weeks, even longer. Consider yourself ahead of the game."

"The game's moving faster than I expected."

"Emma, it's your decision. At this point you aren't committed to anything."

Commitment—something she would never be ready for. But this was business, not personal. "Let's go for it. Your estimate, my visit to the bank." She took a breath, hoping what she was about to say was true. "I'm ready."

Seth met her gaze and Emma wondered if she saw doubt in his expression. No wonder. She wasn't exactly brimming with confidence. Change. Maybe this time she didn't have to run from it.

Randy Carter clicked off his cell phone, then stared at the dull green living-room wall. The pair of faded, bucolic pictures were the same ones his mother had hung nearly thirty years ago. The tired landscapes were the closest his family had ever come to the country.

It wasn't sentiment that kept him from changing the dreary decor. His mother had died long ago, but Randy didn't particularly miss her. She had been a misery, always carrying on about his father, a man who'd left them when Randy was ten, Ken still in diapers. Randy didn't miss his father, either. The old man hadn't wanted the burden of a couple of kids.

There was only one person Randy cared about—his younger brother. No one had messed with Ken when he was growing up, shielded by Randy's heavy fist. And he had passed on a lot of his street sense, but not enough to keep Ken out of trouble.

Ken was young, too young to be sent to a federal pen. But that D.A., that *woman* D.A. wouldn't listen. And now…

Abruptly Randy stood, stalking over to Ken's empty room. Now Ken was hurt. Beaten. And it was bad. Bad enough to put him in the infirmary, the warden's assistant had told him. Bad enough that Ken had been rushed to surgery because of internal bleeding.

No one did that to Kenny and got away with it. Randy didn't blame the inmates. They were burning off the anger being behind bars caused.

It was *her.* Emily Perry. She was to blame. Curling his fingers into a fist he pounded the wall. White dust flew from the destroyed sheetrock. She'd gotten away once. She wouldn't again.

Chapter Four

"This prospectus is very professional," Harry Dodd told Emma. Although he was the sole loan officer, his desk merited a small office in the bank lobby. "A lot of small businesses just have a few scraps of paper they call their records."

Emma couldn't divulge her legal background. "I like to keep everything in order. Which brings me to you today. I've outgrown my current space. As you can see from my figures, the business has grown appreciably since I opened the shop."

Harry nodded. "Impressive. And you own the building?"

"Yes."

"Is there a mortgage?"

"Yes." She'd used a good deal of her insurance money for a down payment, but it hadn't been enough to buy the shop outright. She hoped that wouldn't block her loan.

He didn't seem perturbed, though. "I know the building you're in. The last business there had a good run, over forty years. Maybe with this addition you will, too."

She brightened, scooting forward to the edge of her chair.

Harry Dodd looked up from the papers. "I think we can do business, Ms. Duvere."

Relief made her smile. "I'm so glad to hear that. I think it's a wonderful location and I don't want to move." She hesitated. "The shop means a great deal to me."

"That's the feeling that keeps Rosewood alive. Pride, a sense of ownership in the town. I see you've only been living here a couple of years."

"Yes. Is that a problem?"

"Not at all," Dodd assured her. "I'm encouraged when new businesses choose Rosewood. Big or small." He jotted down a few notes. "I'll run a credit report, but I don't anticipate any problems. I'll draw up the paperwork today."

"That quickly?" she asked, surprised.

"Yes. It's straightforward." He glanced at his desk calendar. "Can you come in tomorrow? I'll need a few signatures, and you can collect your check."

Emma was stunned. It was as though everything had been pushed into high gear. "Yes, that will be fine. Thank you, Mr. Dodd."

He stood, extending his hand. "You'll find that we may be a small town, but we'd like to think we're part of the twenty-first century."

They shook hands. "I've learned that small-town thinking is something to be valued."

Mr. Dodd's expression showed his approval.

Emma was optimistic as she left the bank. It was a clear, beautiful day. On impulse, she walked to her shop.

Century-old trees lined the street, a link from Rosewood's Victorian past to the present. A sprinkling of pedestrians strolled the shaded sidewalks and some cars rolled by. She loved the quiet, the sense of solidity. And the pace. Not frantic, not too sleepy.

Unlike many towns in rural America, Rosewood's downtown thrived. Although the buildings were old, they weren't shabby reminders of better times. They housed vital businesses—the drugstore, an ice cream and soda shop that boasted original marble counters, the hardware store and others.

As Emma examined the hardware window she'd decorated, she shook her head at the changes put in motion since she'd met Seth.

At her own shop, she smiled at the jingle of the bell as she opened the door. Tina was with a customer, but when she spotted Emma she excused herself, practically running across the store. "Well?"

"They said yes."

"Hallelujah! So when does the remodeling start?"

Emma blinked. "I haven't set a date yet since I didn't know what the bank would say."

"Then you need to call that yummy contractor right away."

"Yummy?" Emma echoed.

Tina rolled her eyes. "As though you didn't notice. Fine. Phone that *capable* contractor and see when he can start."

There were times Emma wondered who was really in charge of the shop. But it didn't bother her. It was good to work as a team.

With Tina's eyes fastened on her, Emma stowed her purse beneath the counter and reached for the phone.

Seth answered on the second ring. He was ready to start immediately. She mouthed the word *tomorrow* in Tina's direction. "Okay, then. That'll be great."

Tina crossed to her side in a flash as she hung up the phone. "I can't wait!"

Emma smiled weakly. There was no turning back now.

After a long night, Emma decided she had overreacted. Growth for her business was a good thing. It didn't mean she'd forgotten the past. She'd been forced to move away from L.A. and establish a new life, it hadn't been her choice. Somehow, becoming too successful or happy had seemed like a betrayal, as though she was forgetting Rachel and Tom, leaving them behind.

They deserved more. They were more than painful memories. She thought of her late husband's smile, of baby Rachel's laughter. That's what she needed to remember.

She kept that thought close as she went to the bank. She picked up the check without a hitch. Afterward, she stopped by the bakery for muffins and cookies. Suddenly, it seemed as though a celebration was in order. And she was certain Tom and Rachel would approve.

Humming as she sailed into the shop, her eyes widened in surprise. Seth had already erected the scaffolding. As she walked deeper into the shop, she saw Tina through the open curtain of the back room. The shop wasn't open yet, but there was a flurry of activity.

"Hey, boss!" Tina greeted her, hands filled with a carton. "Yum, muffins. Looks like you got cranberry-orange *and* poppy-seed."

"Yes." Absently Emma placed the muffins on the counter. "What's going on?"

"I thought I'd get started on the things that need to go in the storage unit," Tina replied.

"We have a storage unit?"

"Out back." Tina put down her carton and reached for a muffin. "It's portable."

"I see." But she didn't.

"I started with stuff from the storeroom that we don't use very often. I figured that would be your plan." Tina glanced up from her muffin. "Isn't it?"

"Yes, I suppose so." Dazed, Emma felt helpless in the ebb of change.

"Everything go all right at the bank?" Tina asked.

"Yes. Actually much quicker and easier than I thought."

"Then what's wrong?"

"Tina, you see too much."

"It's a character flaw," she replied, unperturbed. "Did you have other ideas about the storage unit?"

Emma shook her head. "I'm glad you got started. I just…"

Tina pinched a cranberry from her muffin. "You just what?"

"I really don't have a plan. And that's not a very propitious beginning."

Tina frowned. "You drew up a great plan for the bank."

"That was on paper," Emma reminded her.

"We don't work with a plan, and look how good business has been."

Emma returned the smile. It had seemed as though Tina had simply wandered into her shop the first day it opened, but Emma believed the Lord had nudged the woman her way. She was both right hand and friend.

"Everything go all right at the bank?" Seth asked from behind.

Startled, Emma turned. "Yes. It was painless."

"Good. Once most of the storeroom is cleared, I'd like to begin with the addition. When it's completed, we can move the display section farther back and I can work in the shop area."

Emma took a deep breath. "That sounds reasonable. When do you want the back room cleared?"

"As soon as possible. I want to rip out

some of the plaster, examine the bones, see what we have to work with."

That sounded awfully messy, but Emma braved a smile. "I haven't ever had anything remodeled before so I'll trust your plan."

Seth nodded, then retreated to the scaffolding.

Tina sent her an encouraging grin as she pointed toward the front door. "Looks like we'd better open."

Emma was startled to see two customers waiting patiently on the sidewalk. Heavens! She felt as though days had passed since she'd awakened that morning rather than mere hours.

As she hurried to unlock the door, Emma sensed she was embarking on more change than she'd counted on.

After more than a week at the costume shop, Seth felt the days passing quickly, much faster than the evenings here at home.

He had discovered both good and bad in Emma's hundred-plus-year-old shop. Some previous repairs had been done well, others were questionable.

And he found himself thinking too much about the worry that had settled in Emma's expression. He'd had previous customers who worried during the expansion process. But Emma was different. For such an independent business woman, he sensed she was unusually vulnerable.

It wasn't something he'd commented on. He didn't intend to. Despite also being her neighbor, Seth preferred to think of their relationship as strictly business.

Staring into his freezer, Seth wasn't inspired by any of the frozen entrées. And he couldn't face another hamburger. He took out one of the TV dinners, not particularly caring what it was. As he closed the freezer door, he glanced out the kitchen window. A small flurry of movement caught his eye. If he wasn't mistaken, one of Emma's hole-in-the-wall gang had escaped again.

He could pick up the phone, call Emma and let her deal with the dog. Instead, he dropped the uninviting TV dinner on the counter, then headed outside. Sundance dug at the siding of his house. He remembered Emma's mention of mice. Maybe she was right.

Seth squatted down. "What do you have there, boy?"

Sundance spared him a glance, apparently decided he was no threat, then resumed his digging.

"I'm guessing Emma wouldn't be thrilled if you brought home a mouse." Seth considered letting him continue, but dirt was flying into the terrier's white fur. "Okay, Sundance, time to go home."

Seth picked up the dog, which, although startled, didn't growl or try to bite. Chuckling, Seth decided the dog simply looked annoyed. Probably already plotting his next escape.

The gate to the backyard was latched when Seth opened it. No telling where the dog had crawled through. Seth carried him over to the back door and knocked.

Immediately he heard a crash inside, followed by loud, furious barking. He hesitated for only a second. Turning the knob, he called out as he entered. "Emma, it's Seth McAllister. You all right?"

Emma stood by the kitchen sink, shattered bits of china at her feet. But it was her expression that caught Seth's attention. Fear. Not the fleeting kind that said she'd just been startled. This was a sickening fear that still held her frozen.

"Emma?"

Her mouth opened, her tongue moistened her lips, but no sound emerged.

"I'm sorry I scared you." He held up Sundance. "I found him by the side of my house."

She finally focused on her dog. "Oh. I didn't know he'd gotten out...." She pushed the hair back from her forehead. "Um, thank you."

"Sure." Her fear was still visible, eerily real.

She was reaching for control, though. "I'm sorry he bothered you."

Instinctively he knew it wasn't time for a flip answer. "He didn't. I spotted him from my kitchen."

"Oh." She held out her arms and Seth handed her the dog. She hugged Sundance, then looked down at the shards of china on the floor.

"Why don't I help you sweep this up, keep the dogs from cutting their feet." As he spoke, Butch took a protective step to-ward Emma.

"Stay," Emma commanded him.

Spotting the pantry, Seth pointed to it. "Broom in there?"

"Yes, but you don't have to—"

"No big deal." He crossed the floor and quickly located the broom, making short work of the mess. But as he was finishing, Seth noticed a few spots of blood on the floor. He glanced up. "You must have got-ten cut."

"I don't think so."

"It was either you or Butch."

Emma released Sundance, then exam-ined Butch. But the dog wasn't cut.

"Your turn," Seth told her.

"I'm fine," she protested.

He pointed to the kitchen chair. Reluc-tantly, Emma complied. She wore cotton slacks and sandals. Kneeling, he slipped the shoes off her feet and immediately saw the wound.

"It's your heel."

She twisted her foot to look. "No won-der I didn't see it."

"Where's your first-aid kit?"

"Top shelf of the pantry, next to the fire extinguisher. But I can fix this myself."

He rose, crossing the kitchen. "Don't be a hero. That's got to hurt."

"It's okay," she insisted.

But he wasn't convinced. The first-aid kit contained everything he needed. As he applied the iodine, Emma didn't react as if there was pain. But he saw a fair-sized chip of porcelain imbedded in her skin. Using tweezers from the kit he pulled it out. Emma couldn't help flinching.

Gently, he taped the gauze bandage in place. "That should hold it."

She still looked unnerved. "Thanks. I'm not usually so careless."

He shrugged. "You weren't expecting someone to pound on your back door when it was nearly dark. I wasn't thinking. Did I ruin your dinner?"

"No. Just about to start on the salad dressing." She pointed to the counter and a bowl of fresh greens.

"*Homemade* salad dressing?"

The hint of a smile touched her lips. "Have you eaten?"

He thought of the frozen entrée he'd abandoned. "Still working out my menu."

"I have enough for two. Force of habit. I always make too much."

For an instant he wanted to ask why. Had she once been married? Was that why pain lingered in her eyes? Had she loved someone who'd then hurt her? But the moment passed. There wasn't a place in his life for those questions. Or her answers.

Meeting her gaze, Seth realized he didn't have to go there. But he could share a simple meal. "Sounds better than my options at home."

Her smile grew. "Good. I hope you like fried chicken."

Until that moment he'd been focused on Emma and the crash he'd caused. Now he sniffed the air and his tastebuds stirred. "I didn't know anybody still made chicken at home."

She checked a sizzling pan on the stove. "There are a few old-fashioned holdouts who don't go to the Colonel."

Old-fashioned? Emma? Then again, perhaps that wasn't a bad thing. "Can I help?"

"You can set another place at the table. Plates are in the cabinet above the dishwasher."

It was easy to find what he needed. Although her cabinets weren't as lean as his, she didn't have an overabundance of dishes or kitchen tools. She seemed like the kind of person who would own treasured keepsakes from previous generations. Instead everything seemed relatively new.

The bistro-size kitchen table that sat in the curve of the bay window was just big enough for two people. She obviously didn't expect much company. It was covered with a cheerful cloth, but the solitary plate looked lonesome.

She turned toward him, a rueful expression on her face. "I can't eat fried chicken without mashed potatoes. Just one big plate of cholesterol, I'm afraid."

"Doesn't the salad counteract that?"

"Good try," she replied, handing him a steaming bowl.

It didn't take long to dish up the food and they were soon sitting at the table. "Looks delicious."

"Thank you." She put her hands together in a well-remembered position. "Would you bless our meal?"

Seth gritted his teeth, biting back his gut response. "It's your home."

Curiosity flashed across her face but she nodded and then uttered a short prayer. She was too polite to ask, and offered him the platter of chicken.

It tasted as good as it smelled, but Seth was still uncomfortable. And he remained tense, expecting to be quizzed.

Again Emma surprised him. "Do you like dogs?"

He blinked, then looked over at her pair of canines. "Sure."

"Are you thinking of getting one?"

Seth hadn't owned a dog since he was a child. He'd wanted to get one for his son, Davy, but his ex-wife was allergic to them. "Not really. Why?"

"I know Sundance has been a nuisance. And for some reason he's drawn to your yard. I thought if you had a dog he might be content to play through the fence. Now I'm wondering if I should build a second barrier of some sort behind the fence so he can't crawl through."

"There's no need to do that." He saw that the dog was eyeing them with interest, no doubt having recognized his name.

"I don't want to annoy you."

He lifted a forkful of fluffy potatoes. "It's a fair trade. Sundance can roam all he wants if I get homemade fried chicken once in a while."

She hesitated, then nodded. "Deal."

He wondered at her reservation. "Don't worry about the dogs. You're not obligated to any future meals."

She lifted her head sharply, her face suddenly distressed. "I'm sorry. I didn't mean to imply that you're not welcome at my table."

Emma was so contrite, so disturbed that Seth found himself surprisingly touched. "Surrounded by a meal like this, it would be difficult to feel unwelcome."

She fiddled with her water glass. "You can probably tell I don't have a lot of company for dinner. Not that I haven't made friends in Rosewood. I have. Really good ones. Like Tina, who you met." Emma paused. It wasn't that she was out of breath, it seemed. More like she was out of words. Then she glanced down. "But I guess I've become accustomed to being on my own a lot, and not dependent on anyone else. It's easier to stand alone than to get used to leaning." Suddenly she shook her head. "I apologize again. You didn't volunteer to be my analyst."

"I live alone, too."

"Which is a good reason to have a dog. People don't think you're as crazy talking to a dog."

He looked over at the mischievous pup. "I'll keep that in mind."

Her mood had lifted and he wanted to keep it that way. And he refused to examine why. Or to dwell on the notion that she needed protecting.

Chapter Five

The following week passed with astonishing speed. Emma wasn't sure if that was because of the confusion caused by the remodeling.

Or by the presence of Seth McAllister.

He seemed to be everywhere. And because he had to constantly shift things, she kept having to go to him to find what she needed. And each time she forced herself not to think of the evening they'd shared supper, how he'd carefully bandaged her foot.

No one had been that solicitous since her husband had died. And she wasn't sure how to handle it. So far she'd acted as though it hadn't happened. It seemed easier than facing the possibility that she could begin to feel more than neighborly toward Seth.

Even as she processed the thoughts, she denied them. Her husband was gone, so was all that she associated with marriage—the closeness, the vulnerability, the need for that special person always to be there. The horrible emptiness when they were gone. That was something no one told you beforehand.

She remembered the promise that had stretched before her as a newlywed. It seemed as if nothing could have touched them….

Since then pain had been her companion, but she hadn't allowed it to become her friend. And that was more tempting than it would seem, hiding away, drawing on hatred. But she knew that wasn't what the Lord wanted for her.

Still she couldn't believe her path was to marry again, to test the boundaries. Emma shook her head as she looked for a bolt of white fringe. A man ate dinner at her house, an *unplanned* dinner, and she was considering the pros and cons of marriage.

What used to be her sewing area was now covered in dust sheets. And the boxes of notions were stacked high out of reach. "I wonder where the stepladder is," Emma muttered.

"Can I help?" Seth asked from behind her.

Startled, she restrained the scream in her throat. "Just looking for the stepladder. I can't reach the box of fringe."

His long arm easily reached the clear plastic box. "This one?"

"Yes, thank you." Emma could hear how stilted the words sounded and inwardly flinched.

"Yoo-hoo!" Cindy called out from the front of the shop.

Grateful for her friend's interruption, Emma raised her voice. "Back here." Cindy had come to her rescue more than once. She had introduced Emma to the Children's House, a charitable organization Cindy had founded along with her husband, Flynn. Housed where Cindy lived before she got married, the big rambling building was a haven for children. Although Cindy now employed full-time help, she had once run a smaller version of the children's program on her own.

Kids who needed special attention and sometimes foster children without homes came to the warm, welcoming home. And Emma volunteered there. Although the loss of her daughter would always, always cause pain, she had managed, with Cindy's help, to see beyond the pain when she was at the Children's House.

Cindy approached as she usually did, full of laughter and energy. "Wow! The work's coming along!" Then she glanced pointedly at Seth.

Clearing her throat, Emma made the introductions.

"I've heard great things about you," Cindy exclaimed to Emma's embarrassment. But Cindy didn't miss a beat. "I've been trying to convince Emma for months that the shop had to be enlarged."

"Growing pains can be difficult," Seth responded.

"Yes," Cindy replied. "But it's not always possible to keep things the same."

Emma met Seth's gaze and a flash of understanding passed between them.

"I won't stay and add to the confusion," Cindy continued. "We're having a barbecue tomorrow. Can you come?"

"I suppose so." Rattled, Emma tried to concentrate on the invitation. "It sounds like fun."

"Good." Without pausing, Cindy turned her attention to Seth. "You must come, too."

"I'm not—"

"I refuse to take no for an answer," she warned him. "My husband, Flynn, makes a killer brisket and it's not to be missed. And don't worry about getting lost. Emma knows the way."

Seth started to speak.

Again Cindy jumped in before he could. "I know you're new to town and want to get acquainted. Michael Carlson will be there, as well."

Seth's business connection, Emma realized. Which would make it difficult for him to refuse. She withheld a groan. She couldn't beg off, having already committed to attend in front of Seth. Yet apparently it was sizing up to be a party of couples.

And two painfully obvious singles.

* * *

Cindy and Flynn Mallory's contemporary house looked sleek, cool. The Mallorys however were warm, loving—a family that almost hadn't been.

Flynn had been married to Cindy's late sister. And, although Cindy had loved him from afar, she'd never dreamed she would one day be his wife. Together they were raising his triplet daughters, an adopted son and their youngest, a boy born a year after their marriage.

And they entertained often. Although both were busy with business and philanthropic duties, they always made time for friends as well as family.

Friendship had brought Cindy to Rosewood. Katherine Carlson, her best friend, was pastor of the community church. And she had urged Cindy to make a new start in Rosewood when Flynn had married her sister. Now it seemed as though they had always lived in the warm, welcoming town. And Cindy wouldn't want to be anywhere else.

She frowned at the stack of plates still

in the kitchen. Perhaps she hadn't taken enough outside.

Scurrying toward the terrace, she squealed when Flynn reached out, catching her around the waist.

"Whoa! You're rushing around as though we'd never had a barbecue before. What gives?"

She nibbled on her bottom lip, unwilling to spill the beans.

"Cindy?"

"You'd have found out eventually anyway," she muttered. "I invited someone new in town—Seth McAllister."

He lowered his eyes to meet hers. "Should I be worried?"

It was amazing how he could still make her go wobbly with just a look. "Not a chance."

"So who is the victim for?"

She grimaced at his choice of words, then giggled when he kissed her neck. "Emma."

His hands still encircled her, but his teasing playfulness ended. "Is she ready?"

"I think so. I hope so." Frowning, Cindy forgot about the plates. "You know I've always wondered if there's more to Emma's past than she told me."

Flynn stroked Cindy's wild, fiery red curls. "She'll tell you when she's ready. I speak from experience."

Cindy pressed her face against his sturdy shoulder. "I want her to find the same happiness we have."

"You're a one-of-a-kind original," he reminded her.

Feeling his love, Cindy thanked the Lord for her multitude of blessings. Being that blessed made her want to give back in equal measure. It was the impetus behind the children's home she'd founded. And it propelled her to reach out to the lonely. In doing so, she'd made the best friends of her lifetime. Friends she wanted to be just as happy as she was.

Flynn kissed her forehead. "If anyone can make a fix-up work, it's you. Do I have a role in your master plan?"

She smiled. "I suspect that Seth needs friends. He has a lonely look about him." She knew without asking that Flynn would reach out to this stranger. She squeezed his hand as she heard the voices of their first guests arriving.

Before long the well-manicured lawn was dotted with people. Some drifted toward the round, canopied tables, others nibbled at the appetizers or drank cups of the light, frothy punch.

Cindy spotted Katherine and Michael Carlson. Their children immediately mingled with those already playing on one side of the yard that was fenced off for just that purpose. And Katherine deftly wove through the adults to join Cindy.

"Is Emma here yet?"

Cindy swiftly glanced around before shaking her head. "I hope we don't appear as obvious as we sound."

"They're both single. I really doubt this will be their first setup."

"I don't know. He looks wounded, too."

Katherine nodded. "Emma told me she'd invited him to church, but he wouldn't go."

"I thought about Flynn all morning, about what would have happened if he hadn't found his faith," Cindy confessed.

"We don't know why Seth refused to attend," Katherine reminded her gently.

"True."

"Don't worry. You haven't lost your matchmaking talents." Katherine's gaze cut across the yard. "Look at Grace. She's positively blooming."

Cindy harrumphed as she watched Grace and Noah Berry. "That would be because of her husband."

"Who came to you to draw her out."

Cindy shrugged. "Which brings me back to Emma and Seth, neither of whom asked to be drawn to-gether. I hope I did the right thing."

Katherine winced. "I just remembered something Michael said. He wanted to introduce Seth to someone, as well. He mentioned it after they met, but I haven't thought about it since then."

"You don't know who?"

"No. He mentioned it and about that time the kids got into something. And I put the whole thing out of my mind."

Dismayed, Cindy stared at her friend. What if Michael had invited a woman to the barbecue, someone he intended to introduce to Seth?

Chapter Six

Seth closed the door of his SUV after Emma was inside. He hadn't planned on driving her to the barbecue. But then he hadn't intended to go, either. However, it would have been rude to refuse the invitation. And ridiculous to go in two cars when they lived side-by-side.

He used the SUV for his work and usually it smelled of sheetrock or hamburgers. But a subtler, indefinable scent drifted toward him. Emma's perfume, he realized. Strictly feminine.

As Emma was today.

Not worried about business or the remodeling, she looked softer. He'd noticed that right away. Along with the graceful turn of her ankles that peeped out beneath the broomstick skirt. She wore sandals and he was surprised to see that her toenails were painted bright red. He hadn't expected that. Or the light tan of her shoulders. The soft cotton of her peasant blouse draped in easy folds against her skin, and her long blond hair was down, loose. The only jewelry she wore were long, slender turquoise earrings that matched her eyes.

And then he stopped cataloging her attributes. So she was a woman. He'd known that. But it was easier to ignore her when she wasn't sitting beside him.

"Is it far to the Mallorys'?"

Emma shook her head. "No. You'll find nothing's too far away in Rosewood." She looked out the window. "How do you like our little town?"

"It's okay." He turned in the direction she'd indicated. "People are friendly."

She smiled and he noticed a dimple beside her mouth. She hadn't smiled enough for him to notice the charming feature before. "I thought so, too, when I came here. I still do."

It didn't take long to drive the rest of the way. He was surprised by the architectural flair of the Mallorys' house. It was very different from the other homes he'd passed in town. Was there a local architect with this talent? he wondered.

Two large bouquets of balloons were tied to either side of an open gate. The sounds of voices and laughter drifted over the fence in the light afternoon breeze.

It had been a long time since Seth had attended a party. Those had gone the way of everything in his life after he'd lost Davy.

Glancing at Emma he saw uncertainty in her expression. Why? These were her friends, her territory.

She didn't offer any clues as they passed through the gate and into the backyard, where the party was in full swing. Cindy Mallory was easy to spot with her bright red hair. But many of the others became a blur as people greeted Emma and she introduced him.

Within a matter of minutes he received a dozen offers of assistance—for anything he might need to get settled in.

When no one was within hearing, he turned to Emma. "I'm not used to a small-town welcome."

"It can be overwhelming, I'll admit. But they aren't empty offers: Neighbor looks out for neighbor in Rosewood."

He thought of the long, empty months he'd sat alone in his apartment after he and Carla separated, without comfort of any kind. "I'll remember that, neighbor."

Her expression was tentative, almost uncertain. It reminded him of the fearful look on her face that first night in his yard.

He needed to remain detached. He couldn't ask what was wrong.

"I thought that was you," a man said from behind him.

Seth turned and discovered Michael Carlson. "Cindy mentioned you might be here."

Michael smiled. "You couldn't keep Cindy and my wife apart with a crowbar."

Emma chuckled. "That might be true, but I wouldn't phrase it that way in front of them."

"Katherine knows it's true." Michael glanced across the yard toward his wife, an intimate, loving look. He brought his focus back to Seth and Emma. "I see you two have met."

"We're next-door neighbors," Emma explained. "And I took your advice. Seth's remodeling my shop."

There was an unusual gleam in Michael's eyes; he looked at the same time amused and satisfied. "That's great. I suspected you two might be a good fit." Michael cleared his throat. "It doesn't look like you've had a chance to get something to drink. Why don't we fix that?"

Seth nodded. "Emma?"

"Sounds good."

Michael led the way across the yard. "The ladies love the punch." He held up a bottle of root beer. "But this is as sweet as I can tolerate." Coolers filled with ice and all sorts of sodas sat on a table close by.

Seth noticed that most everyone was paired off. Maybe that's what made Emma uneasy. He hated being a fifth wheel. Maybe she did, too.

"Do you play softball?" Michael asked.

"It's been a long time."

"We have a great team, but we always need more players."

Seth considered Michael's importance as a business contact before he answered. "Sounds like fun." A strange expression crossed Emma's face, but it disappeared almost as quickly as it had come.

Michael smiled. "Every once in a while we even win a game." He glanced across the yard. "I'd like you to meet some of the other guys on the team." He glanced at Emma. "You don't mind?"

"Not at all." Emma watched them as they walked away. Did Michael think she and Seth were there as a couple? He'd learn soon enough that wasn't true. A sharp stab of loneliness hit her. Hard.

Swallowing, she glanced around at her married friends. And remembered how warm and wonderful it felt to be part of a couple, secure in that other person's love.

Knowing that wasn't going to happen again made her throat feel tight. She spotted Tina, also alone, and snagged her attention.

"Ah, a kindred spirit," Tina greeted her, then reached for a cup, filling it with punch.

"I *was* feeling the pinch of being the

only uncoupled pair on the ark," Emma admitted.

"I keep thinking it'll get easier, being on my own," Tina said. "But events like this one…"

"I know."

The two stood together, a comfortable silence between them. They'd been friends long enough to understand the unspoken.

"Seth seems like a good catch," Tina commented, too innocently.

Emma was surprised and also unexpectedly dismayed. "Are you interested?"

Tina shook her head. "Nope."

Just what sort of man would interest her friend? "Why not?"

Tina shrugged. "Maybe it's that light in his eyes when he looks your way."

"Now you're being ridiculous."

"Or maybe it's the way you look at him when you think no one notices."

"You have an active imagination." But Emma wasn't annoyed. Her friend was just trying to make her feel better about herself.

"And for a creative person, sometimes yours is a little too inactive," Tina replied.

They shared a laugh as the guests began lining up at the wide buffet tables. It didn't take long to fill their plates.

As Emma looked for a place she and Tina could sit, Cindy caught her attention, waving them over to her table. It soon became apparent why. Seth and Michael, led by Cindy's husband, Flynn, joined them. Katherine, along with Grace and Noah Berry, weren't far behind. The round tables comfortably seated ten, so she and Tina didn't feel as though they were crowding the couples.

Quieter than usual, Emma watched the interplay between Seth and the others at their table. She was gratified to see that the men so readily included him in their circle. Possibly that was her friend's doing.

By the time they ate dessert, Emma was almost sure of it. And she was pleased for Seth. But she was also fairly certain he didn't realize that the softball team he'd agreed to join and now talked about was a church-sponsored group.

Grace Berry sat a few chairs away from Emma. She was the local high school's English and Drama teacher. Once a public relations executive, she had been injured in a horrendous car accident. The plastic surgeon who had rebuilt her face was now her husband.

Emma had gotten to know her while working on costumes for the high school drama club. So she listened when Grace began to speak about the school's production of *The King and I.*

"We have some really talented young people," Grace continued. "And they're so enthusiastic."

"Do you have everything you need for the play?" Flynn asked.

Grace smiled at Emma. "The costumes are going to be wonderful. We're shorthanded on workers to construct sets, though."

Michael glanced at the other men at their table. "You've got able-bodied volunteers here ripe for the picking. Count me in."

"Me, too," Flynn agreed.

"She already has me on music duty," Noah explained.

Emma tried not to be obvious as she gauged Seth's expression.

He hesitated, then volunteered as well. "I'll have to work it in while I'm remodeling Emma's shop."

"Any time you can give us will be greatly appreciated." Grace's wide smile acknowledged all their offers. "And you'll find that the time with the kids is a gratifying experience."

Emma glanced from Grace to Seth, disturbed to see a wealth of pain in his expression. If she'd looked a moment later she would have missed it since he quickly hid the response. Why, she wondered, had Grace's words triggered such a devastating reaction?

Seth was relieved when the evening ended, when he was able to deliver Emma safely home. But at her front door, she turned to him. "Would you come in for a few minutes?"

He hesitated.

"Please?"

He nodded and she turned the key in the lock. The dogs recognized him and didn't bark, pawing in turn at Emma's knees, then at his. The lights in the living room were on, welcoming. It wasn't something he was used to anymore.

"I'll let the dogs out back," Emma told him. "Would you like some coffee? I have decaf."

It wouldn't really matter. He'd be facing another night of elusive sleep anyway. "Sure."

"If you'd like a fire, there are some logs in the basket. And the gas starter's on the right side of the poker."

As she left the room, he stacked two small logs that wouldn't burn more than a few hours. The gas starter made the fire catch quickly.

Seth could hear the quiet rattle of dishes from the kitchen and soon he smelled the freshly brewing coffee. As he waited for Emma, he pushed aside the living-room drape, looking out at the quiet street. He'd come a long way from Dallas. Yet he felt as if he hadn't moved an inch.

Emma's footsteps were quiet, but he sensed her presence and turned to cross to her. He took the tray from her hands, while she pushed the books on the coffee table to one side.

She'd remembered he took sugar, he realized after a sip. Her own coffee was diffused with cream, as he, too, remembered.

Funny, he knew so little about her. It seemed odd that he knew this detail.

She sat beside him quietly for a few moments as they both settled into the warmth of the coffee and the fire. A spark jumped in the fireplace and a moment later, Emma finally spoke. "Can you tell me about it?"

"It?"

"Whatever's causing the pain I saw in your expression tonight."

Great. Now he was an open book. He'd thought he was an expert at disguise. "And you're so sure about what you saw?"

It was Emma's turn to hesitate. She stared down at her coffee. "It's not the first time I've seen the pain…in your eyes. I hope I don't sound nosy—that's not my intent or my reason for asking. But you don't know many people in town yet and I thought you might need someone to listen."

He hadn't wanted to bring his past with him to Rosewood, but maybe it wasn't possible to leave it behind. And something about Emma told him she could be trusted. "You already know I live alone."

She nodded.

"I'm divorced." It wasn't all of the truth, only a small part of his past. But Emma waited patiently. "Carla and I were happy for a good while." He swallowed. "Our son, Davy, became the center of our world." He cleared his throat. "He was six when he died."

Emma gasped, a quiet, wounded sound. She took his hand. "I'm so sorry."

He took a moment, then acknowledged her words with a stiff nod. "Leukemia. By the time it was diagnosed, he was gone so quickly it didn't seem real. I kept expecting to wake up, to find Davy safe and well in his room." He was surprised to see tears in Emma's eyes. Surprised to feel the need to comfort her.

"There's nothing worse than the loss of a child," she told him, her voice quivering. And he suspected the pain he saw in her eyes was more than empathetic.

"After he was gone, Carla and I didn't have much to say to each other anymore." He pulled his hand back, clasped his own together tightly. "And it was too painful for her to have me around. I reminded her too much of Davy, of all we'd lost."

Emma brushed away a tear. "I see why the thought of mixing with kids disturbed you. But it doesn't have to be bad."

He glanced up sharply. Easy for her to say. "You don't know what you're talking about."

Something he couldn't decipher surfaced in her expression. "I'm not suggesting it's easy. But staying away from children is almost worse. It's like building up a dam inside and the pressure hurts more and more."

He stood abruptly. People always thought they knew how he must feel. But they didn't. Not by a long shot. "I know you think you're helping—"

"No." She stood, too. "I'm not sure anyone can."

Seth met her compassionate gaze, startled by the insight. "Then why…"

"Keeping it inside sometimes hurts nearly as much. Children are part of life. You can't avoid them forever. And the kids in the play are in high school, older than your son."

Seth swallowed. He would never have the chance to see what kind of young person Davy would have become, to watch him grow, to learn what choices he would have made. "I'm not sure that makes it any easier."

Emma touched his arm. "Seth, do what you feel you have to. Grace will understand if you aren't able to volunteer. Once you get to know her, you'll find you have a lot in common."

He thought of the welcome Emma's friends had given him. Backing out was ignoble at best. "I'll give it a try. But no guarantees."

The understanding on her face stirred something inside him. Something he didn't want stirred.

Chapter Seven

Most kids weren't familiar with *The King and I*. That was fairly obvious as the string section of the high school orchestra valiantly practiced the notes of the musical's overture. Emma had yet to sketch the costumes and she was trying to reacquaint herself with the show, too. She was also trying, without much success, to corral the energetic teenagers playing the leads.

But she kept one eye on Seth. She'd thought of little else but him after he'd told her his story. That and her own lost child. She longed to tell him about Rachel, that she did know exactly how he felt. It was a loss no one else could truly understand.

But the details of her past were something she couldn't share. At least not if she wanted to stay safe. There were times when that didn't seem to matter, but she couldn't inflict a similar pain on her parents.

She wondered if Seth was close to his mother and father. There was so much she didn't know about him. She'd already discovered that he was an intensely private person. But why had he chosen to move to a town where he didn't know anyone? And why did he constantly intrude on her thoughts?

That question was the most difficult to answer. She ran through a list of reasons—he was her neighbor, new to town, a fellow human in pain. But the truth was she still felt the connection they'd made when they'd first met.

Grace approached, clipboard in hand. "I'm sorry the kids are so wild tonight."

Emma smiled. "Just filled with young energy. You know I don't mind."

"Thank goodness. Some of our adult volunteers aren't so understanding." She glanced toward Seth and Michael. "I hope Seth didn't feel roped into volunteering."

"I think it's helpful for him. He doesn't know many people in town yet, and it's a good way to get involved."

Grace nodded. "It took a lot of prodding for me to join in at first, but I'm so glad Noah and Cindy didn't give up on me."

Grace's severe injuries had been emotionally crippling, but the warmth of new friends and the love she'd found with Noah had turned her life around. Emma hoped Seth would find the same restorative qualities in Rosewood. She couldn't divulge what he'd told her, but she could try and make this situation easier for him. "Seth's a quiet person. I know the guys will make him feel welcome."

"And I will, too," Grace promised. "You didn't know me then, but when I first came to Rosewood I spent most of my time hiding. I thought I'd never fit in. It took a long time to believe I really had."

"I admire your courage."

Grace squeezed her hand. "It's amazing how much inner strength we can all find with the right help."

That's what Emma was counting on. As Grace moved on to handle another mini-crisis with the crew, Emma walked over to the set builders.

Seth smiled as she approached. "Already tired of fitting for costumes?"

"No. Just tired of trying to rein in the kids. What are you working on?"

"The palace." He flashed a rare smile. "It's not looking very royal, is it?"

"Not yet," she admitted. "But I'm confident it will. I'm trying to picture the original Broadway production, but all I can remember is the movie *Anna and the King*."

"You could rent the old fifties' movie version with Yul Brynner and Deborah Kerr," he suggested. "It's one of my mom's favorites. I never stuck around to watch the whole thing. First song, I was out of there."

Surprised and pleased, she beamed at him. "What a great idea! Would you like to watch it with me, at least till the first song?"

His smile turned rueful. "I dove right into that one, didn't I?"

She fiddled with the crinoline fabric in

her hands. "I could probably be persuaded to make fried chicken."

He groaned. "I'd sit through two musicals for fried chicken. Mashed potatoes, too?"

"What else?" she agreed. "Tomorrow?"

"Tomorrow."

Just then, Emma realized there were several children headed their way. She recognized a few from Cindy's shelter. They must be the younger kids playing some of the king's many children, something she'd forgotten about until that moment. Cindy must've recruited them to be part of the community experience.

Bent over the table saw, Seth didn't see the children immediately. Emma swallowed hard. *The kids in the play are in high school, older than your son.*

There was no time to warn him, no words she could say to ease the situation.

"Hi, Miss Emma," nine-year-old Sarah greeted her. "Are you going to be in the play, too?"

Emma would have smiled at that, but she was preoccupied with Seth's reaction. The surprise in his expression was quick, the accusing look he sent her more lasting.

"Miss Cindy said we're supposed to help paint stuff," Sarah explained.

"Don't you have to rehearse?" Emma asked, hoping to steer them away from Seth's work area.

"No, we practice after school, but it's not with the big kids yet."

Emma beseeched Seth with her eyes to understand. "It's been a long time since I saw *The King and I.* I'd forgotten there are younger cast members." Her voice brightened a bit for the small ears that could hear the exchange. "So, it looks like we have some helpers."

Seth finally looked at the children. "There are a few pieces ready to paint."

"That's girl stuff," young Toby said with appropriate disgust.

But the others didn't seem to agree.

"I could get them started." Emma wanted to ease Seth into a reconnection with children, not throw him in the deep end. As quickly as possible, she herded the children away.

She didn't notice that Toby wasn't with them.

But Seth did.

He waited a few moments, ready to get back to his work. The boy didn't budge. Seth swallowed a sigh. "Don't you want to go with Emma and the other kids?"

"Nope."

"What do you want to do?"

Toby small face drew into concentrated lines. His dark eyebrows pulled down and together. Even the freckles sprinkled over his nose and cheeks were scrunched into thought. "Real stuff."

Seth didn't mock the boy's seriousness. "Like what?"

Toby thought for another moment. "Like what you're doing."

A young child and power tools didn't mix. "We only have one table saw. And Michael's using the jigsaw. But I could use some help sanding." He picked one of the small pieces that would eventually be part of the backdrop. "See how the edges are rough?"

The boy's head bobbed up and down.

Seth picked up a palm-size hand sander. "Do you think you're strong enough to sand until the sides are smooth?" He demonstrated the motion.

Toby's puffed up his diminutive frame. "Sure."

Seth located a set of safety goggles. He knelt to adjust them to fit the boy's small face. Unexpectedly, the memory of adjusting Davy's oxygen tube sprang to mind. But as Davy had grown weaker and moved less and less, the tube had laid ominously in place. Clenching his teeth, Seth tried to concentrate on the child in front of him.

Toby fidgeted a bit, then settled down as Seth got the goggles comfortably in place. The mask, designed to cover the nose and mouth, seemed to engulf Toby's face, but he gamely accepted it.

Seth picked up the sander and demonstrated again. Toby's attempt was jerky and rough. So Seth took the boy's smaller hand in his, and showed Toby how to sand the wood smoothly. Just as he'd taught Davy, he thought, and his throat closed.

But Toby didn't notice that anything was wrong. He worked away, ignoring the other kids and the general commotion around them.

Seth went back to his own work, keeping an eye on the youngster. He used to think he would have all the time in the world to teach Davy his craft, to help his son discover his own interests and strengths.

Seth envied Toby's father. Did the man take advantage of every opportunity to be with his son, to interact with and teach him? Where was he today? To be fair, maybe the theater wasn't a place the man was comfortable. Still, it grated on Seth. If he had had just one more day with Davy, one more hour...

"Seth?" Emma's soft voice penetrated his thoughts, surprising him.

He'd been so entrenched in memories he hadn't heard her approach.

"How's it going?" she asked, looking from him to Toby.

"Okay."

She tipped her head toward Toby. "This hasn't gone exactly as I thought it would."

He knew it wasn't her fault. And he had no need to make her squirm. "Yeah. I know."

Her smile was uncertain. "Are we still on for tomorrow?"

Seth's first thought was his work at her

shop. Then he remembered the video and fried chicken dinner. "Sure."

The tension in her expression subsided a bit. "I'm going to help Cindy take the kids back to the home when we're through here."

"The home?"

Emma turned so that her back was to Toby and her words wouldn't carry. "Cindy's Children's House. We can discuss it more later."

Seth looked past her to the young boy. And he couldn't be sure if the knot in his stomach was from his past or Toby's future.

Chapter Eight

Emma was out of the shop the following day with meetings. First with her major client, the Rosewood Community Theater, to discuss the next production. Then with Grace, and finally with a new client interested in window displays.

By the time she'd rented the video and detoured past the grocery store, she was practically running. The busy day had boosted her energy. She was looking forward to her dinner with Seth. Knowing how much pain he was in, she wanted to make sure that she hadn't caused him more.

And despite the frantic pace of her day, she'd thought of little else than seeing him that evening. Not that it was anything more than a dinner with a friend. Still, no other friend had nudged at her emotions with such dogged persistence.

While the chicken soaked in buttermilk, Emma's secret for plump, juicy fried chicken, she arranged a bouquet of fresh flowers. She'd chosen roses for their scent and daisies for their cheerfulness.

Sometimes she wondered if she tried too hard, cared too much, interfered too often. Like now. If Seth wanted his isolation, should she be trying to pull him into the mainstream?

It was just dinner, she reminded herself again. Then why did she have butterflies in her stomach?

Determined to tamp down those feelings, she coated the chicken and put the pieces in the pressure cooker. A few minutes later she had the potatoes cooking, then busied herself with arranging the table. As she put the last touches on the place settings, the dogs barked, ready to come in.

Once they were inside, she fed them so they wouldn't be underfoot during dinner.

As she drained the potatoes, she heard a knock on the back door.

Taking a deep breath, she smiled as she greeted Seth. "Hi."

"Evening." He reached down to pet the enthusiastic dogs. "Hope you don't mind my using the back way."

"No." She was pleased he felt comfortable enough to use the friendlier path.

"It smells delicious."

Absurdly nervous, she turned to the safety of the stove. "I hope dinner lives up to your expectations." She mashed the potatoes with more force than necessary.

"No doubt about it." He reached into his pocket and withdrew two small chewy bones. "Would it be all right to give these to Butch and Sundance?"

Touched by the considerate gesture, she nodded. "They love chewies."

He knelt down, giving one to each. They promptly retreated to separate ends of the room. Grinning, Seth rose. "Can I do anything?"

"Um." She glanced at the counter. "You could put ice in the glasses. The tea's in the fridge."

Emma was disconcerted to learn that her compact, efficient kitchen seemed much smaller with someone working beside her. She hadn't considered that her limited counter space brought two people so close. And despite her assertions, when Seth stood beside her she felt aware...unsettled.

She made quick work of the potatoes, then filled the platter with golden brown chicken. "There's coleslaw in the refrigerator," she told him. "In a blue bowl."

He found it easily and without asking, also located a serving spoon in the silverware drawer. Despite the fact that his house looked as though he were only camping out, he must have known a more comfortable existence. Emma couldn't understand why his ex-wife would prefer being alone with her loss.

Seth reached for the platter of chicken. "Let me put that on the table."

"Fine." Rattled, she tried to remember what else the table needed. Rolls—she'd bought them at the bakery. She reached for the bread basket and filled it quickly.

Sitting across from him, she enjoyed his

appreciation of her efforts. There was something comforting in sharing the intimate space, exchanging tidbits of their day. She missed that so much.

The kitchen was comfortably warm. The dogs contentedly chewed away at their treats, against the hum of the rising wind as it whistled outside.

"Sounds like a storm's coming up," Seth remarked. In the Hill Country, storms hit often without warning. Flash floods filled arroyos, turning them into roaring rivers. It was dangerous for the unsuspecting, but safe here in Rosewood, which had been built on high ground.

"I don't mind storms," she confided. "As long as I feel safe."

"Yeah. They can wreck a construction site, but your shop's safe with the storage shed to block the winds."

Completely distracted by Seth, she hadn't even thought of her store. "Oh! Well, that's good."

"I can go over and take a look if you'd like."

"No!" She calmed her voice. "You don't

need to be out in the weather, either. I'm sure it's fine." For some reason she didn't doubt him. Since she'd been on her own there hadn't been anyone to offer assurances and she'd had to worry about everything herself. It was a relief to accept a bit of help.

When they couldn't eat another bite, they lingered at the table for a while. Then Seth offered to clear the dishes. As naturally, he offered to help wash them. It didn't take long to stack the dishwasher.

Emma filled the sink to wash the pots. She and Seth reached for the first one at the same time, their hands colliding in the soapy water. Startled by the connection, she froze, savoring the feeling of his hand on hers. Glancing up, she saw his eyes darken.

Taking her right hand, he traced the scar on the palm.

Laughing nervously, she pulled it away. "I'll wash, if you'll dry."

He didn't argue.

She reached for the scrubbing pad.

And a crack of thunder rattled the house.

A moment later the lights flickered, then darkened.

It was suddenly quiet, overwhelmingly dark.

Emma waited for the lights to come back on. "It's usually not out for long when this happens."

The expectant silence stretched between them.

Seth broke it. "Can you find a flashlight in the dark?"

She felt her way over to the drawers near the pantry. "It's in here." She switched it on.

"Do you have emergency candles?"

She pulled them from the same drawer, along with matches.

"Where's the fuse box?" he asked.

"Outside. Near the back door."

"Will you be all right in here with the candles while I check the fuse box?"

"Of course." She managed a tiny laugh as she passed him the flashlight. "I'm not a fainthearted female." But as she watched him leave, she felt more than a little faint. He was stirring up feelings she'd put to rest two years ago. Feelings she couldn't handle.

Seth returned within minutes. "Looks like the whole neighborhood's out."

"Oh." She hadn't meant to sound so woebegone, but the thought of spending the night alone in the dark was unsettling. "The lights will probably come back on soon."

"I'm not so sure about that."

"And you're positive it's not just my house?"

"Yes." He paused, straining to see her in the dim light, wondering at the peculiar question. "Why don't I build a fire? It'll light up the front of your house."

"That would be nice."

Hearing the relief in her voice, Seth realized she must be frightened.

The old house had a wide, tall fireplace that took up nearly one wall of the living room. Fortunately she had a large supply of wood.

"You know the fireplace wasn't built just for decoration. A big fire will heat up half the house," she told him. "There's another fireplace in my bedroom. It's not as large but it works as well. These old houses have a lot of advantages over the

newer ones. Besides character, I mean."
The wind whistled loudly. "They're sturdy
in a storm and you can't replicate the
moldings and trim work."

She'd taken to babbling, something she
seemed to do when she was nervous. "The
storm will probably play out by the end of
the night."

She crossed her arms, rubbing them as
though chilled. "Of course. Nothing to be
worried about."

But her body language defied her words.
Her shoulders were curled forward defen-
sively and she looked as though she'd bolt
at the least noise.

"I'll build a medium-size fire. That way
it'll light up the room, but won't eat into
your wood supply if you want to keep it
going."

She nodded.

Which was more indicative of her mood,
her silence or her chatter?

After Seth laid the fire and got it going,
he stood to face her. Immediately he saw
the growing uncertainty in her face and
knew he couldn't desert her. "Do you mind

if I stay for a while? It'll be pretty dark and cold at my house."

Relief filled her face. "Of course not. You're more than welcome. The coffee's probably still hot. Would you like some?"

"If you'll let me help you bring it in."

This time when she nodded it wasn't a stiff, jerky motion. The dogs followed them from room to room as they retrieved mugs of coffee, then rested on the sofa.

Thunder and lightning continued to rail outside and the wind whipped branches against the house.

"It's funny," Emma mused. "I get so used to the hum of the refrigerator and all the electronics. It's startling how quiet the house is without them. Or would be without the storm."

"That's why I like camping. My father used to say it was the only place quiet enough to hear what he was thinking."

She smiled. "Did he take you often?"

"Yeah. He was big on family trips."

"You were close," she guessed.

"Yes."

"Sounds like he was a good father."

He could see the questions in Emma's

eyes. Ones she probably wanted to voice but thought she shouldn't. He sighed. "You want to know about Davy."

"Only if you want to talk about him. I feel so badly about the kids at the high school."

"I know. And it's not realistic for me to think I can avoid children the rest of my life. After all, they're not Davy. There'll never be another Davy."

She was quiet. When she spoke her voice was low. "No. Each child is unique, never to be repeated."

He'd expected a pep talk, not her somber agreement. "Most people think I should move on, have another child. It's not like getting a new puppy after losing a dog. A replacement. A replacement child."

Emma's eyes filled and her lips quivered. "People mean well. They just don't understand and they never can unless they lose a child of their own."

"Davy always lived in the moment. Unlike me. I was thinking ahead, planning on Little League, what schools he would attend. And the time he had…it passed so quickly." He unfurled his fingers, looking into his empty hand. "And now there's nothing tangible left."

Emma hesitantly took his hand. Her touch was gentle. "He's here…in your heart. And that won't ever fade."

Neither would the pain. He studied the fire and listened to the storm's gathering intensity. Evidently it wasn't going to play out quickly.

A clap of thunder shook the house with astonishing force and Emma shivered. Spotting an afghan on the end of the couch, he spread it over her lap.

"We can share," she suggested, pulling the soft wool so that it covered them both.

Seth knew he should probably head back home and turn in for the night. But Emma looked so vulnerable, he couldn't bring himself to go yet. As the fire dwindled, he added a few logs. After a short while he watched as her eyelids drooped and her head slid to rest on his shoulder.

It had been a long time since he'd shared a stormy night, secure from the elements, warmed by a decent fire. Emma's hair fell over one eye. Ever so carefully he tucked it behind her ear. Her glossy blond hair was soft to the touch. Giving in to the temptation he traced the outline of her cheek. It, too, was soft.

He felt so protective toward Emma. He knew there was no man in her life. She never spoke of her parents, or of any family. It was as though she'd landed in Rosewood totally alone with even less past than he wanted to admit to. And while he recognized that Emma was a capable, independent woman, he could see that the layers beneath the surface weren't as solid as she tried to present.

Emma stirred, her face troubled even in sleep. He smoothed the blanket up over her shoulders and she settled beneath his comforting touch.

The log would last through the night. Seth made sure the doors were securely bolted before he left. Everything seemed safe. Everything except the emotions she stirred. And his need to wipe the pain from her troubled expression.

Chapter Nine

By noon Emma still felt flushed. Embarrassed to wake up and realize that Seth must have watched her fall asleep, then tucked her in, she felt like a fool. He was gracious, insisting he'd rested as well, that the fire had kept him from a cold night. But he was only being polite.

What had she been thinking? She'd had her guard up for two years. Why had she let it down with him? Her situation made it imperative that she remain constantly vigilant, alert for danger. But like a well-fed baby she'd slumbered through the night.

It amazed her that she'd been able to. What was it about Seth that made her trust him? Because she did. Subconsciously and now consciously. Was that wise? After darting from shadows for so long, she was no longer certain what was wise.

The whole town showed signs of the storm. Emma's discomfort went unnoticed, and the shop was slow. It seemed everyone was cleaning up their homes or businesses. There was nothing serious, other than a few partially damaged roofs, but limbs, leaves, trash and shingles were scattered over every square foot of town.

Seth had been right. Her shop was undamaged. But they had plenty of cleanup. She and Tina swept and collected trash all morning. Seth had picked up the few heavy limbs that had fallen. After sawing them into manageable lengths, he'd loaded them in the back of his SUV. Unaccustomed to having help with traditionally male jobs, Emma felt the luxury of having Seth help.

Emma cautioned herself not to become used to it, but she knew she would miss him once he met someone, someone who could share his life. She ignored the unexpected pang of regret as she and Tina bagged the last of the leaves in front of the shop.

"That was some night," Tina commented, tying the strings of the trash sack together.

"Yes," Emma remembered. "It was."

"You're unusually quiet. Anything wrong?"

"No." Emma wished she could tell Tina all about the evening, the confusing emotions it had evoked, the reasons why she could never become involved with Seth. But, of course, she couldn't tell anyone about that. "Probably just tired."

"I wore myself out trying the light switches all night. I always say I'd like a night with no distractions so I can read, really relax. Have you ever tried to read by candlelight or flashlight?"

Emma smiled. "Not since I was a kid, when I was supposed to be asleep."

"Trust me. It's not the same. All I got was eyestrain and a headache. I like to think of myself as capable of surviving in a wilderness if I had to. I couldn't even survive in my own living room. I can't believe it—I don't even own a manual can opener. Some survivor."

"Well, fortunately you aren't likely to be stranded on a raft here in town."

"True," Tina agreed. "But it still played havoc with my self-image."

"So, what are you going to do about it?"

"Buy a can opener," Tina replied matter-of-factly.

Emma laughed. "If only all problems could be solved so easily."

"You have a problem, boss?"

Automatically, Emma shook her head. "Just theorizing."

"How's this for a theory? Isn't it great to have someone help out with the heavy stuff around here?"

"Just what I was thinking."

Tina sighed. "He's *still* yummy."

"You make him sound like baked goods with an expiration date."

"Now *that's* a thought." Tina shook her head. "I think I'll sort fabrics while it's slow. Unless…?"

"There probably won't be any customers. Why don't we close up early? Get our yards cleaned up, too. Besides, we've been putting in long hours. And I still have to go to the high school later."

"You want me to help with that?"

"I can handle it." Emma grinned. "You have a can opener to buy."

"And a bigger, brighter hurricane lamp. Okay, no arguments from me. My yard *is* a mess. Besides, I'm exhausted from all that relaxation last night. Call me if you change your mind about needing help."

"I won't, but thanks." Emma breathed in the sweet air the storm had left behind. No longer ripe with the scent of rain, instead it held the smell of new growth, of fresh beginnings. She turned away so Tina couldn't see her face. Fresh beginnings. If only that could be.

The following afternoon Cindy herded her small group of children into the high school. They were excited about being part of the play. At least most of them. She cast a worried glance at Toby. And as she did he took off like a shot.

She sighed, knowing it would do little good to call him back. He was determined to thwart any authority. But he wouldn't roam far. At least he hadn't yet. She was afraid that would come as he grew older.

In his short stay with her, Toby had remained reserved, detached.

She saw Emma entering the auditorium and raised her hand in greeting.

Emma detoured, heading her way. When she reached their aisle, she greeted the children before they scattered. "I'm guessing being in the play is a big hit with the kids."

"Most of them."

Emma followed her friend's gaze and saw Toby, apart. "Problem?"

"I'm afraid so. Not that I can blame Toby. He hasn't had much to get excited about for a long time."

"How did he come to be at the Children's House?"

"His mother dumped him on her sister on her way through town. The grandmother, who lived with them in Dallas and took care of Toby, had died. I'm guessing that could be why the mother skipped out—she no longer had a built-in babysitter. The sister she left him with is divorced and can barely manage her own kids. There's also a boyfriend in the picture who doesn't want her to keep Toby. That's why he's at the Children's House now. I was hoping that the boyfriend might fade from the picture and Toby could be with what's left of his family."

"No such luck?"

Cindy shook her head. "And I'm beginning to feel that even though his aunt is family, it might not be the best situation for him."

"What about his father?"

"Gone before he was born. He's not even listed on the birth certificate. So that's a dead end."

As they watched, Seth set up his tools, Toby trailing behind him.

"Hmm," Cindy murmured. "I noticed that Toby attached himself to Seth the other day. I'm surprised to see he's doing it again."

"Why?"

Cindy's expression was thoughtful. "It's not that Toby's a bad kid. But he resists attachments. Understandably. And he doesn't want anyone telling him what to do. He's young enough that it's manageable now, but I worry it'll get worse."

"Perhaps he's drawn to Seth because he senses he's unattached, as well."

Cindy nodded. "Could be. I'd begun to think Toby might never warm to anyone. I've tried to work with him. Flynn and Michael have, too. But he's closed off."

"He's probably afraid adults will just let him down since that's all he's known."

"I've considered that, too. He stays to himself at the House, doesn't interact with the other children, either."

Emma's eyes filled with tears. "That's so disheartening."

"I'm sorry, Emma. I didn't mean to dump all that on you."

"Why not? You're trying to save him. What could be more important?"

Cindy put her arm around Emma's shoulder and gave her a hug. "You're right, of course. But your tender heart's betraying you."

Emma ran a hand through her hair. "It is?"

"Yes. I think you're like me. I want to take them all home."

Emma let out a nervous breath. "Oh, yes."

What wasn't Emma saying? Cindy had always felt there was a great deal of pain in Emma's past that she hadn't shared. "Has Seth ever thought about being a foster parent?"

"What?" Emma's voice sounded strangulated.

Cindy made her friend look her in the face. "Are you sure you're okay?"

"Yes, I'm fine. Why don't we track down Grace and see what she's thinking about the costumes?"

"Okay." But Cindy wasn't sidetracked. Seth McAllister. What if he was the answer to her prayers about Toby? She was determined to put Toby in a good home. Perhaps the Lord had led Seth to Rosewood for just this reason. One thing was certain. She wasn't giving up on Toby. Which meant Seth wasn't going to escape her radar—no matter how much Emma tried to distract her.

Seth was surprised when Toby latched on to him again. He figured the boy would grow bored, find something else to interest him. But Toby wasn't to be dissuaded.

Seth tried not to, but still compared the boy to Davy. They weren't the same age, of course. And their temperaments couldn't be more different. Davy had always been cheerful, smiling, filled with laughter. Even as a baby. People had commented about his wide grin, his open acceptance of strangers. Seth couldn't forget he'd thought that might become a problem, that Davy could become a kidnapping target.

"Do you gotta nail the pieces together?" Toby asked, holding up two of the cutouts.

"After they're sanded." But not with a nail gun. He didn't want to risk a misfire with all the kids around.

"Okay."

"You sure you wouldn't rather be painting?"

"Nah. That's baby stuff."

Seth wondered about this child with such a tough attitude. "Oh. I thought it was *girl* stuff."

Toby didn't look up, instead putting more pressure into his sanding. "Yeah."

The kid must have something bothering him to be trying to hide it so well. But Seth didn't press.

As they worked, the women of the PTA

set out snacks for the volunteers. Deciding after a time that his little helper needed a break, Seth turned off the jigsaw.

"Whatcha doing?" Toby asked, watching Seth remove his goggles and mask.

"I don't know about you, but I need a break."

"I can keep on working," the boy insisted.

"How about keeping me company for a few minutes? The work will still be here."

Toby debated this. He pushed up the goggles and pulled off his mask. "I guess so."

Seth was careful not to smile. Instead he walked casually toward the folding table with the food. Although he wasn't much of a sweets eater, he picked up two cupcakes, hoping to encourage Toby to fill his paper plate. The boy was on the thin side, but he didn't look undernourished. And from what Seth knew of Cindy, he suspected she wouldn't let the kids in her shelter go hungry. Still, he felt better when Toby picked up some cupcakes, as well.

Seth guessed the auditorium seats wouldn't be too comfortable, so he led the way to the wide steps at the side of the stage. Making sure they were out of the traffic path, he sat, leaving plenty of room for Toby.

Gamely Seth bit into the blue icing dotted with sprinkles. "Did you ever wonder what flavor blue is?" he asked after swallowing.

Toby put his finger into the icing, tinting his skin blue. "It tastes vanilla."

"You like vanilla?"

"I like chocolate better."

"Me, too," Seth agreed. "But the vanilla's growing on me."

"Vanilla can't grow on you," Toby replied with childlike logic.

"I don't know," Seth replied. "Your fingers are turning blue."

Toby shrugged thin shoulders. "That doesn't count."

Seth tried to remember what did count in a child's world. "So, do you hang out at Cindy's very often?"

"I live there."

The blunt answer rocked him. What had happened to the boy's parents? "Do you like it?"

"It's okay." Toby kept his eyes on the floor.

They finished their snack in relative quiet. Seth knew Toby wouldn't appreciate any platitudes, and he wouldn't feel honest offering them.

At the rear of the auditorium, Seth saw Emma standing with Cindy. Both women were watching him. And he had an uneasy feeling that their interest wasn't casual.

"We'd better get back to work." Seth stood, gathering paper plates and napkins.

Toby imitated the man's motions, then followed him back to the jigsaw.

Safety gear in place, Seth finished a few more pieces. He held up the last one, inspecting the edges. "What do you think, Toby? Do you like this shape?" He picked up another one. "Or do you like this better?"

For a moment the boy looked uncertain—something he'd camouflaged before. But he struggled past the hurdle. "The first one."

Seth studied it a bit more. "Yeah. Me, too."

Toby looked at him for another few moments as though trying to see if Seth was humoring him. Then he pulled his goggles back on.

As he did, Seth's determination to remain detached cracked.

Chapter Ten

Two busy weeks passed with Emma caught up in work at her shop and volunteer duties. But not so busy that she didn't notice Seth and the progress he was making on the remodeling....

The addition, framed in and sealed from outside elements, was beginning to take shape. Seth worked quickly and efficiently, not distracted by the surrounding commotion.

Emma wished she could say the same. She still found plenty of time to be distracted by Seth.

It seemed wherever she turned he was there. Working at the shop, building sets at the school, in his yard when she was home. The only place she didn't see him was at church. And he steadfastly refused her invitations to join her there.

Which made her wonder how the evening was going to turn out. It was time for softball practice. And Seth had agreed to play when Michael and Flynn had asked. But he still didn't know it was a church team.

Emma had no doubts everyone would make him feel welcome. But she didn't want him to feel as though he'd been tricked. She wanted to help him heal, not push him farther from his faith.

Shading her eyes from the late-afternoon sun, she watched his tall figure as he ran to catch a fly ball. Naturally athletic, he caught it with ease. He seemed to stand out on the field with his distinctive, handsome features. His strength was evident as he tossed the ball to the pitcher. In his T-shirt and jeans, his tanned arms appeared to be solid muscle.

Absorbed by him, she didn't notice Cindy until she sat down beside her. "Enjoying the view?"

Emma tried to deflect the course of the conversation. "I wasn't sure you'd be able to make it."

"Hmm. So how's Seth doing?"

"He seems to be a natural."

Cindy lifted her eyebrows. "So I see. I wasn't sure he'd agree to come once he found out it was a church team."

"Michael didn't get a chance to tell him at the party."

"Did you?"

"I thought once he saw how friendly the team is and enjoyed himself…well, I thought it might not matter."

Cindy's carefree smile was gone. "Emma, if he's not comfortable with church events, he won't appreciate the subterfuge."

Emma winced. "That makes it sound so deliberate."

"Which is probably how he'll see it."

"I haven't wanted to probe about his faith." Emma guessed that losing Davy had distanced him from the Lord, but she couldn't betray his confidence and tell that to Cindy.

Emma looked out at the field, studying the enigmatic man who dominated her thoughts. She knew Cindy was right. She had to tell Seth before he was bombarded with the information as he had been with the kids at the play.

By the time practice wound down, the sun was dipping low in the sky. Even then the diehard players groaned, hating to stop. But most of them needed to get home to their families.

Seth opened the passenger door of his car for Emma. "Are you hungry?"

"Now that you mention it, I didn't have time to eat dinner."

He glanced down at his casual clothes. "Is there anyplace in town besides the Burger Shack that'll let us in dressed like this?"

"Yes. We only have one upscale restaurant." She paused. "Well, upscale by Rosewood standards. But there's another one that has great food."

"And no paper hats?"

She laughed. "Not a one. Just head to Main Street."

Settling behind the steering wheel, Seth drove away from the ball field. It didn't take long to reach the small downtown.

Emma pointed out the café. It was a cheerful, casual place with the best pie in town. No instant or frozen food. And yet the best thing about it was its unchanging face. The original Naugahyde booths lined the tall, wide windows. Crisp, starched curtains were always impeccably white and fresh carnations filled each bud vase. It was the sort of place that encouraged you to linger over the delicious coffee.

They selected a booth. The menus were tucked behind spotless napkin holders and they each reached for one.

Seth studied the menu a few moments, then looked up with a smile. "Does everything here taste as good as it sounds?"

She returned his smile. "Sure does."

"Too bad I didn't know about this place when I moved here. I wouldn't have had to live on fast food."

Emma's smile faded. If he had they wouldn't have shared those first dinners. She studied the menu even though she knew it by heart.

"Something wrong?"

She was becoming too transparent. "Just

having a hard time deciding what to order."
She settled on soup and salad.

Seth did, too. Along with a steak and
baked potato. "You sure you don't want
more than that?"

"The soup's filling," she replied.

"I want to buy you dinner, to thank you
for all the suppers you've cooked for me."

How neighborly. Still, she smiled
gamely. "Thank you. But soup and salad
is fine for dinner."

"Oh, I didn't mean tonight."

Startled, she lowered the menu. "No?"

"I thought we could go to the one fancy
restaurant in town you mentioned. When we
haven't just come from softball practice."

"Oh?" Like a date? she wanted to ask.
Or still as a neighborly thank-you?

"You don't have anything against *upscale* restaurants, do you?"

She smiled at his emphasis. "I guess *upscale* and *Rosewood* don't really sound
right together."

"I don't know. But it's nice to see you
smile again."

Embarrassed, she fiddled with her silverware. "I've been smiling."

"Off and on."

Not wanting to go there, she tried to change the subject. And decided to take the plunge. "Actually, I've been wondering how to tell you something."

"You're not planning to fire me from the remodeling job, are you?"

She didn't smile.

"Are you?"

"Of course not." She took a deep breath. "I just didn't want to spring something else upsetting on you."

He frowned. "You'd better spit it out."

"The softball team…well, it's a church team."

"And?"

"And?" she repeated. "There's no *and*. You don't deserve to be blindsided again."

His shoulders visibly relaxed. "I found out it was a church team at the practice."

"You did!" Deflated, she stared at him. "And you didn't say anything?"

"Such as?"

She opened her mouth, then closed it again. "I know you don't go to church, and…" Truly lost for words, she floundered.

"But I have nothing against the people who do," he replied quietly.

She had to ask. "Your not going…it's because of Davy?"

He nodded. "He didn't have to die. I prayed for help and it didn't come."

She covered his hand with hers. "Seth, we can't always understand—"

"I know the dialogue. I've offered the same words to friends over the years. But it's different when He fails an innocent child."

Emma desperately wanted to share her own experience, her belief that his healing would come more quickly if he leaned on his faith. But they were surrounded by other diners and she couldn't risk a chance they'd overhear. So she said the one thing she could. "I'll continue praying for you."

"Continue?"

"I've been praying that He'll take some of your pain."

Seth didn't make a move or say a word, watching her with an undecipherable expression.

Afraid that he thought she'd crossed a boundary, Emma waited.

"It's rare to find a woman who cares enough to pray for you," he said finally.

That wasn't what she'd expected.

The waitress served their dinner, then pieces of lemon meringue and coconut cream pie. But Emma didn't taste any of it. She continued to think about his choice of words. *A woman who cares...* Was that how he thought of her? If so, it begged the obvious. Did he in turn care about her?

At the high school, more than a week later, Seth hammered a piece of wood in place. Toby hadn't appeared yet and Seth worried about the boy. Ridiculous, he knew, but he couldn't shake his concern. It was just as he'd expected—being around children opened up old feelings, leaving him vulnerable. That was something he hadn't intended to let happen.

Like his growing feelings for Emma.

He'd been crazy to let himself feel anything for Emma, and hadn't mentioned taking her to dinner again. To make it worse, she hadn't either. She'd simply let him off the hook.

And that made him feel like a heel.

But she didn't need to be involved with a burned-out wreck of a man. And that's what he was. Damaged beyond repair, he could never give Emma what she needed. It was clear she belonged in a traditional family with a loving husband and kids. And neither was in his future.

But each time he remembered that she was praying for him, it unsettled him all over again.

Seth spotted Michael headed his way. He turned off the noisy saw and lifted his goggles.

"Don't you ever stop working?" Michael greeted him.

Seth grinned. "I was thinking the same thing about you."

"Comes with the territory—being the pastor's family. I'm so used to it I don't really think about it anymore."

"Is it hard being married to a minister?"

Michael didn't seem to mind the blunt question. "There are times I wish I could escape with her to a deserted island so we could have more time alone. But that's not the kind of woman Katherine is. And helping out the community sets well with me. Like anything worth having, we work hard to make personal time for ourselves and the kids."

"Sounds like a winning formula."

Michael looked thoughtful. "Someone making you think about marriage?"

"No." The answer was automatic, but the word left Seth empty.

"Fair enough. Actually I just wanted to thank you for joining the softball team. We've lost some of our players lately, not enough time to juggle families, work and the team. Single players tend to be more reliable."

Seth shrugged, ignoring the sting of Michael's reminder. "No problem."

"We pretty much roped you into volunteering here, too. Hope it's not too much."

"No. I don't have any other demands on my time."

"Right." Michael studied him for a moment. "I've noticed that Toby keeps sticking close to you when he's here."

"He's an okay kid."

"I think so, too. But I couldn't get through to him."

Seth drew his brows together. "You tried?"

"He's one of the kids from the Children's House. Cindy's been worried about him, so I tried to draw him out. Fell flat. Flynn tried as well. Zip."

A little kid with a tough attitude. "I was just wondering if he's okay," Seth said. "He didn't show up with the others."

"He has a short attention span," Michael mused. "Could just be that. There's probably nothing wrong."

"Yeah."

"I can find out for you, give Cindy a call."

Seth didn't want to care more about this child. But he couldn't refuse. "Whatever you think."

Michael nodded and turned away.

And Seth put more concentration into the set-building than it required. It beat thinking about another little boy.

Chapter Eleven

Designing costumes for *The King and I* should have been relatively easy. But Emma was struggling. She didn't want to simply copy the movie, beautiful as it was.

Picking up the video, she slowly shook her head. She and Seth had never watched the show together, had forgotten it because of the storm. Emma couldn't bring herself to watch it alone, when she'd planned to share the movie with Seth.

His invitation to dinner hadn't materialized. Emma wondered if he'd been put off by her questions…or simply by her. Perhaps it hadn't been caring she'd glimpsed in his eyes. Perhaps he resented her attempts to help, to talk to him about his faith. Perhaps both.

She tried not to be hurt. People often mentioned events in passing that didn't materialize. It could have simply been a casual idea. She'd been foolish to attribute more to it than that.

She'd plunged herself deeper into her pending designs. And for the last two weeks that had worked most of the time. Seth was still at her shop every day, but the place was always filled with people, and both she and Seth were busy enough to not connect often.

And Emma had avoided going to the school. Until now. She needed to consult with Grace.

Entering the auditorium, Emma braced herself. She could hear the sound of electric power tools on the stage and despite her resolution she immediately scanned the area. She spotted Michael, but didn't see Seth. Frowning, she hoped he hadn't deserted the production because of her.

She walked down the side aisle toward the stage.

Michael noticed her and lifted a hand in greeting.

Waving back, she climbed the wide, shallow steps to the stage. "Hi."

He turned off the saw and pulled down his face mask. "Hey there."

Emma hated to ask. "Isn't Seth helping you tonight?"

"Not exactly."

Emma tilted her head in question.

"He'll probably be here in a few hours."

"Oh."

He hesitated. "Toby's sick and Seth's visiting him."

Her eyes widened. "He is?" She tried to marshal her thoughts. "Is it serious? Toby, I mean."

"Bronchitis. He'll be all right. But he's had to stay in bed. So Seth's been going by there every day."

Wow. "I'm sure Toby appreciates that."

"It's hard to tell with him, but Cindy thinks so. He starts watching the clock about an hour before Seth usually gets there."

She pictured the tough man and the tough-acting child. Perversely, they inspired a tender image.

"You look surprised," Michael commented.

"I am," she admitted. "I didn't know Seth wanted to get…that involved."

"A good man can't look away from a child in need."

She completely agreed, but Michael didn't know how much courage it took to overcome the protective instinct to stay detached. "You're right. And Seth's a good man."

Michael watched her closely. "Also a lonely one."

She didn't feel right divulging what Seth had told her about his past, so she couldn't tell Michael how correct his observation was. "Sometimes we're all lonely. Thank you for telling me about Toby. I hope he'll be well soon."

Michael took the hint. "Sure. How are the costumes coming?"

"Slowly," she admitted. "Haven't quite gotten my inspiration yet."

"You will."

Despite her worry, she smiled. "You sound very sure."

His smile was kind. "Remember, I've seen your designs."

She returned his smile. Grace called her

name then, and Emma turned away, grateful for the distraction. Even though she remained busy the rest of the evening, Emma had more than enough time to notice that Seth didn't appear.

By the time Emma arrived home she was tired. Butch and Sundance jumped up, pawing her legs, wanting attention before they went outside. She had let them out that afternoon when she fed them, but she hadn't had time to play.

Petting them and promising treats, she walked into the yard with the dogs. It was a quiet night, but then it was usually quiet in Rosewood. The moon, high in the sky, bounced soft light over the tall pine trees. It was the kind of night that didn't scare her as much. Not like the dark, inky nights that hid any trace of movement.

"Emma?"

Jumping, heart in her throat, she scrambled away from the voice.

"Emma," Seth repeated, catching her arm. "It's me. I'm sorry I scared you. I was trying to let you know I was out here before you were startled."

Too late. She tried to quiet her wild breathing. Fear still caused her to tremble.

Seth muttered under his breath, then pulled off his jacket, putting it around her. "I should know better than to come up to a woman alone in the dark."

"It's not your fault." The words might have been more convincing had her voice not quivered.

He put an arm around her shoulders. "Why don't we go inside where it's warm?"

She nodded and he guided her to his back door. Butch and Sundance, alerted to his presence, trailed them inside.

"I'm surprised they didn't bark," he muttered, shutting the door behind the dogs.

"They know you, so..." Her voice trailed off. Embarrassed, she tried to pull herself together.

But Seth didn't seem to notice, shepherding her toward the living room. His furniture was sparse, so he sat her in the desk chair before adding a log to the fire. Then he disappeared for a few moments, returning with a blanket that he tucked around her.

"Is it too late for coffee?" he asked, still kneeling, his gaze level with hers.

She doubted sleep would come that night so she shook her head. "No. I'd like some."

He left again and she tried to calm her nerves. But they were still raw when he came back with two steaming mugs.

"My pantry's not as well stocked as yours," he said, handing her one of the mugs. "But it's hot and strong."

Taking a sip, she enjoyed the heat of the coffee.

"Is it helping?" Seth asked.

"Yes." She lowered the mug. "I feel so silly."

"Don't."

She considered arguing, but could see by his face that it would do no good. "I hope Butch and Sundance aren't getting into anything."

"They're exploring. I don't own anything that can be hurt."

Except his heart.

"Emma, what are you so frightened of?"

She wanted to tell him. More than he would ever know. "I didn't expect to see you out there."

"Not tonight. It's something deeper, something that made you react that way."

"My nerves are on edge."

"Why?"

She fought to sound convincing. "I've been under more stress than usual. The expansion, extra business and of course, the costumes for the school play."

He didn't look as though he bought it.

So she rushed on. "Speaking of which, I didn't see you at the school tonight."

"No." He stood, pacing toward the tall, wide window that dominated the wall, then staring out into the darkness. "I didn't make it there."

A different sort of fear seized her. "Toby isn't worse?"

"No." He paused for so long she wondered if he would add anything else. "It's not that. In fact, he's about well. Just has a little cough. He's back in school, though."

"But it has to do with him?"

He turned. "I should've expected you to know that."

She waited.

Seth crossed the room, dropping onto

the stool beside her. "Do you know about him…his situation?"

"Yes."

"How can someone throw away a child?"

She didn't have the answer. But she knew he didn't expect one.

"I keep thinking about the injustice. These people have their child and don't want him. I would have given the world to save Davy and…"

Emma fought her own painful memories. "Toby's lucky he has you."

"Me?"

"Michael told me you've been checking on Toby while he's sick. It sounds as though he's never had that kind of concern before."

"He needs his parents, not a stranger."

"You're not a stranger. Not anymore."

His face was somber. "But I can't be anything more. You know why."

Emma swallowed. It would be easy to dispense some pat advice. But Seth and Toby both deserved more. "You can be his friend."

"That won't help him."

"From what I've seen and heard, it already has."

Seth looked at her hard. "I'm not sure I can keep being his *friend*."

"Because you're afraid you'll get too close." The words slipped out before she could stop them.

"He's already had too much disappointment in his life."

"Which is why he'll take it that much harder if you disappoint him."

Seth turned back to the window.

In the silence, Emma could think of nothing to add. Or how to ease his difficult decision. Again, she'd put her advice between them. Seth hadn't wanted to volunteer at the school. But she'd talked him into it, convincing him it would help. And now...

Despite the fire warming the room, her chill returned. Worse than her fear of the unknown was her fear that she'd pushed him even further away.

Chapter Twelve

Seth's muscles ached. He'd begun work at Emma's shop that morning as soon as it was light. The shell of the addition was nearly complete. It wouldn't be long until he opened up the main body of the shop. But today he was glad to be hammering exterior boards in place. He needed to clear his head and he'd chosen not to use a nail gun, hoping the physical exertion would help.

But his thoughts wouldn't leave him alone.

He hadn't slept the previous night, Emma's words tormenting him. After getting her safely home and making sure she'd locked up, he'd been left to digest what she'd said.

That and her fear.

He couldn't forget the image of Emma's ashen face, her genuine terror. Why wouldn't she confide in him? He'd trusted her with the details of his past. But clearly she didn't trust him.

Between his questions about Emma and his concern for Toby, Seth hadn't felt so unsettled since his divorce. What was he going to do about the kid?

Despite Toby's assurances that he was fine, Seth read the relief in the boy's eyes when he visited. Toby quickly hid it. And that only made it more heart-wrenching.

It was hard enough being alone as an adult. But to be nine years old and have no one… Seth pounded on the nails with extra force.

What would Davy have thought of Toby? Davy had considered all of his classmates as friends, but could he have connected with a child so different from himself?

In comparison with Davy, Toby's life had been a series of abandonments. And from what Michael had told him, even when he'd been with his mother, she'd had no time for him. Too young when she'd become pregnant, she hadn't wanted to be a mother. Toby's grandmother had doted on him, but she'd died.

Seth's own carefree childhood included two parents who were still married to each other and loving grandparents, now passed away. His biggest worry had been making the best Little League team.

Cindy certainly provided all the material comforts these homeless kids needed, but it was an interim remedy. Some of the children would eventually be returned to a parent, some needed counseling, others needed special attention…but Toby needed to find a permanent home.

Seth reached for another plank of wood. From his vantage point on the ladder he could see down to the main intersection. Rosewood was supposed to be his haven, his escape. He knew there were abandoned kids in the city, too, but there, they hadn't been right in his face. Funny how a problem didn't seem to be yours when it was impersonal.

Seth pulled the hammer from his tool belt. But then, maybe this small, involved community would find a home for Toby, one with the two parents he deserved.

Yeah, and the tooth fairy would bring the kid nuggets of gold.

The physical labor wasn't helping. He could pound in a million nails and it wouldn't shake his thoughts.

Emma and Toby.

He wanted to protect Emma from whatever frightened her. The previous night, even though she'd pulled no punches, he'd hated to leave her alone. He'd checked her house through the night and her lights were on each time.

His memory of comforting her through the storm when the electricity had gone out was always close. She'd felt right sheltered beneath his arm, as though she belonged there.

"Seth?" Emma called.

He nearly dropped the hammer. Recovering, he climbed down to ground level. "What's up?"

She held up a cordless phone. "Cindy's on the phone."

"What does she want?"

Emma shrugged. "I don't know. But she did say if it's not convenient to talk right now, you can call her when it is."

"It's okay. I'm already down the ladder." Emma didn't quite meet his eyes. Maybe she was thinking about the previous night, too.

She handed him the phone, then turned away, heading back inside the shop.

Cindy was friendly but quickly came to the point. Toby wanted to go with the other kids to the high school that evening.

"Is he well enough?" Seth questioned.

"I think so. But I won't be able to watch him the entire time, and I don't have anyone else to send along. I hate to ask, but unless you feel you can keep an eye on him I won't be able to let him go."

Concern and obligation tugged at him. "Yeah, I can watch out for him."

Cindy's relief was palpable. "Thanks, Seth. I'm sorry to impose, but Toby hasn't taken to anyone else like he has to you."

Which didn't bode well for the child. Seth kept the thought to himself as he said goodbye. But it stayed with him, unbidden, unwanted and completely unshakeable.

More than two weeks later, Emma was still keeping to herself. Well, as much as she could, considering Seth worked in her shop each day.

He was busy, she knew. After working all day, he still volunteered at the high school. Despite her resolve not to, she had dropped by there a few times, covertly watching him with Toby. Secretly, she hoped that Toby could touch Seth's heart and open it again.

Not that she believed Toby could replace Davy. Her heart ached at the thought. That wasn't possible. No one could ever replace her Rachel…her baby. But she was determined not to be bitter about children. It was one reason she volunteered at the Children's House.

But she hadn't done that as much in recent weeks. Legitimately, she was under a crush of work, but in truth, it was difficult now that Seth and Toby were coupled in her thoughts.

At her kitchen window, Emma tried not

to stare at Seth's house. Not sure if he was home, she didn't want to appear to be snooping…or gazing wistfully.

How had he so effectively crept beneath her defenses? Those emotions were supposed to be buried along with Tom.

Yet her feelings for Seth were growing. She could no longer pretend her concern was simply that of a friend. But it seemed that was how he felt.

Reaching to tilt the blinds, she paused. Was that Sundance digging in Seth's yard? Oh, no! She and her pets had been one major pain to him since he'd moved in.

Practically running, she left her kitchen. The gate was closed but obviously it hadn't stopped her dog.

"Sundance! Stop that!" she called.

The dog ignored her. His short, strong legs continued digging, throwing dirt into the air as the hole deepened.

As she reached him, she heard the distinctive sound of Seth's back door opening. Hiding a groan, she reached for Sundance. His legs continued moving as she lifted him in the air. Barking, he demanded to be let down.

"Been busy, haven't we?" Seth asked, his expression as droll as his voice.

Sundance barked in reply.

Emma grimaced. "Sorry about that. I don't know why he's so fascinated with your yard."

Seth's half grin lifted his lips. "Yours has too much grass. My yard has more dirt."

She dusted Sundance's wiry coat. "And he's wearing a good portion of it. I'll fill the hole back in."

"No need. As soon as he gets out, he'll be back at it. Maybe there's a prehistoric dinosaur bone down there."

"More likely a bone some other dog buried."

"Didn't you tell me the last people had a dog?"

"Yes." She shifted Sundance in her arms. "An older Irish setter. She wasn't as active, but she liked to play with them."

"Which is why Sundance thinks he should be able to come over at will," Seth speculated.

"Probably. Still, I'm sorry he bothered you."

"Did I say I was bothered?"

It was difficult not to be drawn in by his dark eyes. "No, but then you wouldn't."

"I remember getting pretty out of sorts the first time I saw him and you out here."

The memory flashed between them. Suspicion and fear had dominated that meeting. Now Emma looked at him with different feelings.

"Emma—"

Butch barked loudly from the gate and Sundance wriggled to get down.

Emma stood patiently, hoping Seth would finish his sentence. But he didn't.

Groaning inwardly, she wished her pets could have behaved just long enough for her to hear what he would have said. "Well, I'd better see about Butch."

He nodded.

She was aware that he watched her as she walked back.

Resisting the urge to turn around, she went inside. "Sundance, what am I going to do about you?" It was embarrassing. What if Seth thought she used Sundance to get his attention?

Since terriers were bred to dig, Emma

had provided a place in her yard for Butch and Sundance. It was covered with clean sand, and she occasionally hid a dog treat beneath the top layer. And so far, her dogs had been content with digging only there. Now, it seemed that Sundance was addicted to Seth's yard. And she could hardly add a digging area there.

But she could plant something! Something attractive that would at the same time put off her dog. Emma glanced at her watch. The local nursery should still be open. Before she could talk herself out of it, she grabbed her purse.

At the nursery, Emma strolled down the aisles. She wanted a bush with a strong scent to deter Sundance, but not one with any sort of thorns or stickers that could hurt her little Westie.

She thought of Seth's backyard. There was plenty of green in the yard, but not much color. None of the trees or bushes were flowering ones. And the neglected beds hadn't seen flowers for some time.

She decided on three lovely, scented gardenia bushes. As she headed her flat cart toward the cash registers, she was dazzled by colorful pots of chrysanthemums. Unable to resist, she added some to the cart. Geraniums were next, followed by flats of marigolds and petunias. Then she threw on bags of planting mulch.

Refusing to think about the purchases, she paid for them and loaded them into her car.

Back at the house, she carried the bushes over first. With the garage door open, she retrieved her garden tools. Hoping Seth wouldn't discover her until everything was planted, she started first with the hole Sundance had dug. Probing in the dirt, she found the bone that Sundance must have scented.

Setting it aside, she prepped the hole for the transplant. When it was ready, she loosened the freshly watered roots in the plastic container. The gardenia bush looked lonely. So, Emma began digging the second hole.

Until a shadow fell over the new plants. "You and Sundance both feel like digging today?"

Relieved to hear the humor in his voice, she kept working. "I felt I owed it to you after he messed up the yard."

"That explains *one* gardenia bush." Kneeling beside her, he reached for the spade she wasn't using. "Looks like you bought three."

"It looked pretty pitiful all by itself. Plants look good grouped in threes."

"I'll have to defer to you."

Emma sneaked a glance at him, then concentrated on the soil mix. But her gaze flicked back to him. There had been so many things she'd become accustomed to doing on her own. It would be so easy to get used to sharing them.

That wasn't a good idea. Still, she savored the companionship, the sense of him kneeling beside her, working side-by-side with her. Much stronger than her, Seth quickly dug the two new holes.

Emma began patting the soil mixture in one. Seth helped and their hands strayed together in passing. Although it lasted only seconds, she held her breath at the thrill of his touch.

Too soon, the bushes were planted.

"These look great," Seth declared, leaning back to get a better view.

"They'll be prettier as they grow and bloom."

"Provided Sundance lets them stay," he reminded her with a droll grin.

She held up the bone she'd uncovered. "I think this was what he was after. So, fingers crossed, he'll leave them alone."

"Looks like we're done here."

She grimaced slightly. "Actually, I went a little overboard and bought a few other plants. I hope you don't hate flowers. I tried to think of ones that were masculine, not that I'm sure any flowers are masculine. But at least I didn't choose pansies. They *really* aren't masculine. What do you think? Oh, you probably wouldn't have planted any flowers—"

He placed two fingers over her lips to still them. At the same time he grinned. "Let's see what you bought."

She hesitated as they walked toward her garage. *Overboard* was an understatement. Thoroughly embarrassed, she lagged behind.

Seth was bent over the flowers. "Which ones are for me?"

Good question.

Embarrassing answer.

"Actually…" Her newfound flow of words dried up.

He twisted back toward her. "These aren't all…" He waved at the flats of flowers.

Emma cleared her throat. "I'm afraid so. I really meant to just buy one bush. But it didn't look right by itself. Then I saw the chrysanthemums and the rest, well…by then it didn't seem to be so much. It looks like more here in the garage than it did at the nursery," she offered weakly.

He chuckled. "Can't you use some of these flowers?"

"Not really. I planted bulbs early. And the perennials are blooming." She felt like a total fool. This was worse than sending flowers to a man. Decorating his entire yard—what had she been thinking?

"You're going to have to tell me how to plant them," he said, with easy acceptance. "And let me pay for them."

"But Sundance—"

"Didn't dig up my entire yard." He picked up the flats of marigolds. "Can we start with these?"

Because of his attitude, she smiled as

well. "If you're sure you don't mind having flowers."

"Careful or you'll talk me out of them."

Her smile widened. "Yes, we can start with those."

Side by side, they prepared the beds. Although neglected, they hadn't been taken over by weeds.

Emma pushed back her hair, then reached in her pocket for a band, pulling her hair into a ponytail.

Seth watched her. "You look like a teenager."

She felt the warmth of a blush.

He traced the line of her cheek. "I didn't know women blushed anymore."

Emma stared down at the marigolds. "Afraid so." Embarrassed, she rambled. "But then I'm hopelessly old-fashioned. I like Victorian houses, cooking, gardening. I can even tell you that I picked these marigolds because they repel mosquitos. They give off a subtle odor that mosquitos don't like. But luckily, the gardenias will smell good. I didn't get any roses because of the thorns. And even though I hope the plants keep Sundance from digging over here, I don't want him to get stuck on thorns."

Seth chuckled.

"Surely you don't think it would be funny for an innocent little dog to get hurt on a rosebush?" she said.

"Of course not. I'd debate the term *innocent* when it comes to Sundance, but that's not why I laughed."

"It's not?"

"Nope. It's you."

Embarrassed, she again felt her flow of words dry up.

Seth lifted her chin so that she met his eyes. "I'm not laughing *at* you. I wish you could hear what I do. It's good, Emma. Very good." He held her gaze so long it seemed that even the breeze paused in anticipation.

And when they resumed planting, Emma could still feel the force of his gaze like a physical caress. Like the kiss she longed for.

Chapter Thirteen

The flowers were thriving. And each time Seth stepped into his yard he thought of Emma. How could he not? Was it somehow possible she didn't know how appealing she was? Her animation, her enthusiasm, her compassion: they had reached through his pain, through his determination to keep her at bay.

They reached him as much as the terror he'd seen in her eyes. If only she'd tell him what she was so scared of.

He knew she'd taken pains to check on Toby since they had discussed him. A woman like Emma—unmarried and childless? She had so much to give a child.

He had, too. Seth remembered the first time he'd set eyes on his son. Davy had been perfect from his very first moment.

Seth pushed the thoughts away. He was determined to remain upbeat today. He and Emma were taking Toby fishing. Completely recovered from his bronchitis, Toby was having a hard time containing his energy.

So Seth had decided to take him on an outing. But he wasn't sure about caring for Toby on his own. He also didn't want Toby to misunderstand, think that Seth would become his foster parent. Emma had offered to make lunch.

Rosewood's lake was a quiet place. Ringed by forest, it hadn't changed much over the past hundred years. Rowboats and small fishing boats, powered by equally small outboard motors, were the only water traffic. A well-worn walking path followed the curve of the shoreline and a few picnic tables were scattered beneath the branches of tall pine trees.

When Seth had first seen the lake it made him think of a time capsule, perfectly preserved from decades earlier. Because of the noise ordinance, it was quiet enough to hear the splash of water as an occasional fish leaped over the surface, then disappeared.

Toby was pumped. There was no other way to describe it. Unaccustomed to individual attention, he was about to burst. Seth had borrowed the boat from Michael for the day and Toby's eyes had widened when he saw it. For once, his tough exterior wavered.

More affected than he wanted to be, Seth hid his emotions as he stowed the gear in the boat. Entrusting the live bait to Toby, Seth smiled at the boy's glee.

Michael had outfitted them with appropriate poles, as well as life preservers.

Michael had become a friend, Seth realized. Faster than he could have expected, his ties to the community were taking root.

With everything loaded, Seth offered a hand to Emma. Her touch, along with her smile, curled his toes. It was her smile that teased his thoughts when he wasn't with her. Hers was a smile that warmed him during the lonely nights.

"Seth!" Toby shouted.

Jarred from his thoughts, Seth made sure Toby didn't turn over the boat as he leaped on board. Once they were all safely seated, Seth steered the boat to a shady area.

"How come we're not staying in the sun?" Toby asked, tugging on the new baseball cap Seth had bought for him.

"Because the fish like cool water better," Seth replied, turning off the motor.

The subsequent quiet was that much more pronounced. Soon Toby's chatter filled it, though. Seth showed him how to attach the bait to the hook and drop the line in the water. Then he turned to Emma. Without asking, he baited her hook.

"Aren't you gonna fish?" Toby asked him.

"Sure. Just have to get my line baited."

Several minutes passed and Toby glanced at Emma. "Can you feel anything on your pole?"

She shook her head. "Nope. How about you?"

He scrunched his face in deep thought. "I thought maybe I did for a minute."

"Could be a fish is nibbling on your bait," Seth told him.

"Then wouldn't I have a fish?"

Seth smiled. "Not necessarily. Some of them will take little bites of the bait instead of swallowing the hook."

"We could check," Emma suggested. "I think I felt the same sort of thing."

"Is that okay?" Toby asked Seth.

"Sure," he replied, catching Emma's small smile, quickly hidden.

She and Toby pulled in their lines.

"Yeah. My bait's almost gone," Toby announced in disgust.

"Me, too," Emma commiserated. "Could I talk you into baiting my line, Toby?"

"Yeah! I mean, sure, okay." It was clear Toby was pleased to be asked.

Toby plunged his hand into the bait bucket and Emma made an appropriately disgusted expression.

"Ick!" she exclaimed with a shudder.

Toby looked at her, then shared a grin with Seth.

He grew serious again, making sure he selected just the right bait. And he took great care with the slippery worm, fastening it on Emma's hook.

"Thanks. I'm not much on worms."

"Girls are like that," he told her.

Seth and Emma fought smiles.

Then they were all quiet.

Until Toby felt a tug on his line. He nearly jumped out of the boat in his excitement.

Seth talked him through reeling in the small fish. By the time it was in the boat, Toby was ecstatic.

"First fish of the day," Seth praised him. "Way to go."

Toby looked slightly abashed. "Thanks."

"Congrats, Toby!" Emma chimed in. "Are you *sure* you haven't been fishing before?"

"Uh-uh. Honest!"

"With a start like this, you're going to be quite the fisherman," Emma told him.

Seth felt an assault of emotions as he watched Emma and Toby. She was so warm, so giving, so natural. It was a gift.

Emma was so different from his ex-wife. Carla hadn't been cold, but it also hadn't been in her nature always to give without expecting anything in return. Despite whatever troubled her, Emma had a sweetness. Not one she put on when convenient, but one that was part of who she was.

She would be a wonderful mother.

The unbidden thought rocked him, not because it was new to him, not that he hadn't thought it before. But because he connected the feeling with Toby. Emma could give Toby the kind of attention he needed.

"Seth, can we eat my fish for lunch?" Toby asked him, barely keeping his seat in the boat.

Seth glanced from the small boy to the very small fish. "We didn't bring wood for a fire. And I think Emma made us a really good lunch. She's a great cook."

Toby considered this. "Okay, I guess. When are we going to eat?"

"I'm thinking you're hungry." Seth reeled in his line.

"Uh-huh."

"Emma?"

"Starved," she assured him.

Once the poles were stowed, Seth steered the boat to shore. As he tied up the boat, Emma got Toby to help her with the lunch hamper and jug of lemonade.

"My grandma was gonna bring me to a park like this, but her legs didn't work too good," Toby confided. "And she couldn't breathe without her oxygen tank."

Seth placed an arm over Toby's shoulders. "Sometimes it's hard for old people to do all the things they want."

Toby nodded.

Seth tightened his grip.

They picked a table beneath tall oak trees that grew beside even taller pines. Toby helped Emma spread out a cotton tablecloth. She ruffled his hair when he asked if they *had* to put their sandwiches on the paper plates she'd brought.

"We have ham, chicken salad or peanut butter and jelly," Emma said. "What sounds good?"

"Chicken salad, unless you or Toby want it."

"Peanut butter and jelly," Toby broke in. Then he glanced up at Seth. "Please."

Emma's face told Seth that the child was melting her heart.

She pulled the sandwiches from the hamper, along with a plastic container. "Potato salad," she explained.

It didn't take them long to polish off the sandwiches. As he'd expected, Emma brought out homemade dessert. "I hope you like brownies, Toby."

"I like *everything* chocolate."

"Me, too," she agreed, smiling, holding out the plate. "Seth?"

He took one of the brownies just as a few fat ducks waddled toward the table. "How do they always know when to show up for dessert?"

Emma laughed. Then she reached back into the hamper.

"Don't tell me you packed duck food in there, too?"

"Sort of," she replied. "Extra bread to go along with some extra chicken salad." She pulled a slice from the plastic bag and handed it to Toby.

"How do they eat it?" he asked.

Seth met Emma's glance. Such a simple, common thing. But in the city apparently no one had ever taken Toby to see the ducks. "Just tear it into pieces about this big." He held up two fingers. "And toss the bread to them. Don't hold on to it and let them eat from your hand."

"I'm guessing this isn't out of the ordinary for them," Seth commented, watching as Toby fed the appreciative ducks. "They probably never have to forage for their own food."

She laughed. "It's unlikely."

Seth got up and stretched. "I don't know about them, but I could use a walk to burn off some of that lunch."

"Good idea. Why don't we pack everything up first, put it in the car. Keep any other little forest creatures from checking out the menu."

"Animals?" Toby asked excitedly. "Like bears?"

Seth and Emma both laughed.

"I don't think so," Seth replied. "Raccoons, squirrels, rabbits, that's probably about it."

Toby looked disappointed for only a moment. Then he brightened. "Maybe we'll see some up real close when we're walking!"

Seth chuckled at Emma's expression that said she wouldn't be all that pleased. It didn't take long to stow the hamper and jug, then start on the walking path.

"I think that one duck is glaring at us," Seth commented.

"Ducks can't do that," Toby replied.

Seth raised his eyebrows and shrugged his shoulders. "If you say so."

Distracted by a sturdy stick that stuck out from the undergrowth, Toby bent and tugged on it. When it wouldn't come free, Seth placed his bigger hand next to Toby's and helped him yank it loose.

Acting as though the simple piece of wood was a trophy of war, Toby swung it by his side as they hiked.

As the path wound back around the lake, Seth led Emma and Toby through the low grasses toward the shore. "I'm itching to skip a stone."

Toby tilted his head. "A stone?"

"Want to help me look for some? Flat ones work the best."

Intrigued, Toby started searching the ground. It didn't take long for him to find several small flat rocks.

Seth demonstrated, skipping the stone past the shadows, into the glossy, sun-brightened water that stretched out to the middle of the lake.

"Wow!" Toby was visibly impressed.

Seth chuckled. "Now it's your turn."

It took several tries before Toby made a rock skim the surface a short distance. Seth and Emma cheered his efforts, but he wasn't satisfied.

"I want to be able to make it go as far as yours!" he said, tilting back his head to look at Seth.

"You'll get it. It'll just take practice," Seth reassured him. "Then one day it'll go the distance."

Toby threw another stone, imitating Seth's stance and motion.

As he did, the boy's grip on Seth's heart grew that much stronger.

Chapter Fourteen

In the following days Emma couldn't shake the look on Seth's face from her mind. Considerate, tender…pained. She knew how difficult it was for him to watch Toby, knowing how much the child needed a home.

She was having the same difficulties.

And there was nothing she could do to help Toby. She couldn't minimize the possible risks. Although she'd had no trouble since coming to Rosewood, she couldn't play with a child's life. He needed security, stability, things she couldn't offer.

The bell on the front door of the shop tinkled as Cindy opened it.

Always glad to see her friend, Emma

smiled as she greeted her. "Tell me you've come to rescue me with a lunch invitation."

Cindy smiled ruefully. "Maybe tomorrow? Actually, today I've come to talk to Seth."

Emma gestured to the back. "Sure. He's in the addition."

She knew Cindy's visit must have to do with Toby. Knowing the scars on Seth's heart, she wanted to tag along with Cindy to act as a buffer. It struck Emma that her concern for him had crossed a line. The need to shield him from more hurt, the wish to make him happy...they were deep feelings. Despite her belief that she could never have felt this way for a man again...she had. She did.

And for once the past didn't overshadow the present. Her thoughts were filled with Seth. In his quiet, strong way he had entrenched himself in her heart.

The minutes passed painfully slowly as Emma waited for Cindy or Seth to come out. The shop was quiet, with few customers to distract her. Not that there wasn't plenty of work. She had dozens of costumes to make. But it was difficult to concentrate.

She was ready to jump out of her skin by the time Cindy walked back into the shop. Her thoughtful expression was hard to read.

"Everything okay?"

Cindy's expression was noncommittal. "Talk to him, Emma."

Immediately Emma's gaze darted toward the addition. Then she looked back at Cindy. "Thanks. I will."

After Cindy left, Emma turned the shop over to Tina. Bracing herself, she approached Seth. His back was to her.

"Seth?"

He glanced around. "This won't get finished if I keep getting interrupted."

"Please?"

She heard him sigh before he turned to face her. "How is it I know you're here for the same reason Cindy was?"

"She asked you, didn't she? About being a foster parent for Toby?"

He nodded.

"What did you say?"

His gaze sharpened. "I think you know."

"Oh, Seth." She crossed the room, stopping close enough to catch his arm. "This isn't what you want."

"Now you know more about that than I do?"

"Seth, I know that you're consumed with pain over Davy. And you're scared to get too close to Toby, afraid that you won't be able to face the pain if anything happened to him."

"You think you know." Seth's voice took on an edge. "But you don't. You can't."

She tightened her grasp on his arm. "That's where you're wrong. I *do* know. I wish I didn't." Despite her efforts, Emma's voice had begun to tremble. She tried to get it back under control. "I've never told you about my past. And I have my reasons why. But I can tell you this... I had a child as well, a little girl. She was barely two when she died. And there's no greater pain in the world." She closed her eyes against the tears.

Seth put his arms around her. "Emma, why didn't you tell me before?"

That she still couldn't answer. She rested against the comfort of his strong shoulder.

When she finally pulled back, he stroked her hair, tucking some strands behind one ear. "Then you know why I had to say no."

"Why you *think* you have to say no. Toby needs you. He already looks up to you. Other people have tried with him but no one connected, no one until you. He's chosen you, Seth."

Seth looked uncertain, torn.

Gently she stroked his face, gathering her courage. "Seth, what if this child were Davy? And he had no one to reach out to him?"

Anguish darkened his eyes. "What if I fail him?"

Her fingers rested on his cheek as she lifted her gaze to meet his. "That isn't possible."

He hesitated. "That's a lot to live up to."

"Not for a good man, one who's strong, who cares."

Seth bent his head. "You have a lot of faith in me."

Her heart hitched. "More than you know."

Light spilled through the tall, slim windows. It seemed to erase the last shadows in Seth's eyes.

And when his mouth met hers, it erased the final doubts about him in her heart.

The hours flew by as Seth prepared for the new addition to his home. To that end he decided he needed more than survival basics in his house.

So he enlisted Emma's help. She brought over many of her own things, insisting she had enough to share. And she'd shopped, one of his least favorite activities, for other items to soften the house. With his approval, she'd added a comfortable sofa and chairs in the living room along with rugs to warm the wood floors.

"I'd like to build his bed. Not just the standard headboard and footboard, but something more unique."

"And not too babyish," she agreed.

"Or all blue. I want it to reflect his interests. Only thing, I don't really know his interests."

"He enjoyed fishing."

Seth shook his head. "Not crazy about a fish theme."

She grinned. "Me, either. Just thinking aloud."

"He likes building things, working with his hands." Seth picked up a sketch pad and pencil. He quickly roughed out a design. "What do you think?"

"A construction zone?" She chuckled. "Definitely appropriate. We could use some of those great bright colors like construction yellow and splashes of neon orange. Too much and he'll never be able to get to sleep in here."

"I'll work on the bed design. Maybe add a climbing wall, too."

"Ooh, I like that. And maybe a window seat with storage for toys or tools, depending on which he likes best."

"I haven't bought him either," Seth realized.

Her smile was both tender and teasing. "And that's okay. If you start with the basics you can add things as you learn what he likes."

"I guess." He turned around, sizing up the room. "I think I'll build in the desk, give him plenty of room for homework. Even though, when I was a kid, my mom had me work on my homework at the kitchen table."

"Which will probably happen some of the time, too, with Toby. Those are the details that'll work themselves out over time."

"You seem awfully sure."

"I'm sure of you, Seth."

Putting down the sketch pad, he picked up her hand, again tracing the scar on the palm. "Do I deserve your trust?"

She nodded tremulously.

Seth wanted to ask her more, but he didn't push. It hadn't been long since he'd thought she kept her secret because she didn't trust him. And not that long ago that he'd believed he would never open his heart to another child...or woman.

"I couldn't do this without you," he said.

Her eyes filled with emotion. "You could. But thank you for letting me share."

He kissed her forehead and pulled her close for a moment. "I wouldn't have it any other way."

As she pulled back he recognized the pain in her expression.

"What is it, Emma?"

But she was shaking her head. "Just thinking of how much we have to do to get Toby's room ready. If you trust me to choose a paint color, I'll run over to the hardware store."

"I trust you, Emma."

Again that indecipherable look surfaced in her eyes. "Good. I'll get started then."

In a sudden flurry of motion, she hurried from the house. Escaped, he corrected himself. She hadn't left, so much as she had escaped.

Still, she had to return soon. They had agreed to finish the room by the end of the week. That way he could bring Toby home Friday afternoon, and he'd have the weekend to settle in. And to his relief, he knew that meant Emma would be back soon.

The rest of the week was jammed full. Emma had helped Seth paint the walls. She'd created window coverings and a bedspread, and together they'd revarnished the floor.

But the masterpiece was the bed Seth created. He'd built it from clear acrylic with black, lacquered trim. Assembled, the bed looked like a large pair of safety goggles. She'd never seen anything like it and knew Toby would be impressed. Taking Seth's cue, she'd bought other clear acrylic accessories, pegs for his backpack and hats as well as shelving.

The splash of colors warmed the room, not conflicting with the techno statement, but keeping it human.

When Emma inspected the room after it had been put together, she noticed that Seth had added a computer. He'd obviously built the desk with one in mind since it had all the right compartments. There was a small television with a built-in DVD player as well. He'd also hung a hard hat on one of the clear pegs. Emma had resisted the urge to add a collection of stuffed toys, tucking only one, a small teddy bear, beside the pillow. She knew that even a boy with as much bravado as Toby needed the comfort only a teddy bear could offer.

And she had volunteered to cook for them. Now that Friday had arrived, she was as nervous as Seth. He had checked and rechecked Toby's room. She'd barely been able to convince him to wait until school was out to leave for the Children's House to pick up Toby. Cindy had said she would have Toby all packed and ready by five o'clock. By three, Seth was ready to bolt.

"Maybe I should have bought one of those things for playing video games," he muttered.

"In time," she replied. "He's going to be overwhelmed as it is."

A new worry surfaced in his face. "Too overwhelmed?"

"No. It's just right. It's obvious you put thought and care into the room. He'll love it."

Pacing, Seth glanced around. "The living room looks good, thanks to you. And I like the kitchen table."

"I'm glad. I thought it would suit you."

"You sure we bought enough groceries? I haven't kept the fridge stocked very well."

Patiently she smiled. "You have enough to last at least a week. You couldn't stuff any more food in there."

He opened the pantry, obviously cataloging the contents. "You think we got enough snack food?"

"Enough to rot all of his teeth."

Seth still looked worried.

"Kidding, Seth. It's fine. And we can find out what Toby likes to eat, see if he has any favorites."

"Yeah." He stared into the pantry. "What if he can't get to sleep tonight?"

"He's not a puppy being separated from the litter," she reminded him gently. "What did you do if Davy couldn't sleep?"

"Read to him." A look of panic crossed his face. "But I don't have any books for kids!"

Emma had purchased two, which she'd placed on the shelves. But it might be a way to divert Seth. "There's a great children's bookstore downtown. The lady who owns it knows all about kids. She can tell you what nine-year-old boys like to read."

He checked his watch.

Emma hid her smile. "You have plenty of time. You don't have to pick up Toby for two hours."

"Right, okay. And you think that's a good idea?"

Looking at him she felt her heart quake again at his generosity and concern. "Yeah, I do."

Absently, he kissed her cheek. "Okay, then I'll be back right after five."

"Fine. If you don't mind, I'll hang around till then. I have a few things to get ready."

"Oh, I want you to be here. You're here for dinner, right?"

This time she didn't stifle her grin. "Yes, I'll be here. Now go."

After he left, she started collecting the ingredients for chocolate chip cookies. She wanted the house to seem cozy and inviting and few things said cozy like freshly baked cookies. Tina had volunteered to run the shop, drafting a friend to help in case it got too busy.

Emma planned on making homemade corn dogs and French fries for dinner. She hadn't met a kid yet who didn't like them. She'd thought she would leave Seth and Toby alone this first day, but Seth had insisted. And he'd been grateful when she'd suggested cooking.

It was such a little thing. Seth had made the major leap, accepting Toby into his home. Toby was a lucky child. Instinctively Emma knew that Seth's would be a big love, one that would make Toby feel secure and wanted. Blinking back tears, she knew that she could have searched the planet and not found a more genuine and honorable man.

She might tell him so. But then she'd be obliged to tell him everything. And knowing could only endanger him. And that she'd never do.

In the past week, despite the excitement of helping Seth fix up his house, Emma had also been worried. She wanted to assist Seth as much as possible, but she couldn't become more involved with him or his new life with Toby. Young and innocent, Toby would be a perfect target. She had to distance herself, not in one huge abrupt move, but it would have to be done.

Emma longed to call her mother, to tell her about Seth, her conflicting feelings. In addition to being against the program's rules, it was possible her parents' phone was being tapped. The D.A.'s office had never been able to prove Carter was behind the arson and murders, so he was free.

Free to strike again when he chose.

She was determined to make every moment of this special day count. She had prayed for Seth and Toby. And their miracle was happening. She didn't want to cloud that in any way.

She watched the clock impatiently as the cookies baked, anxious to see Toby's face when he arrived in his new home.

Just after five-thirty she heard the car in the driveway and rushed to the front door, opening it wide. Next door she could hear her dogs barking.

"Can I help?" she asked, seeing Toby and Seth each carrying a bag.

"No, we've got it," Seth replied.

A strangely quiet Toby nodded in agreement.

"Hi there, bud. Welcome."

Toby toed his tennis shoe in the grass. "Thanks."

Emma could see that he was afraid, even though he liked Seth and no doubt wanted to be here. She knelt to his level. "Do you like chocolate chip cookies?"

Distracted, he nodded.

"Whew! Good thing. I just baked about a zillion. Think you might want to help eat a few?"

"I guess so."

She glanced up at Seth who looked worried.

"Would you like to see your room first?" she asked gently.

Toby nodded again.

Emma stepped back. "I'll let Seth show you the way."

Timidly Toby followed Seth. When they reached his room, Seth stepped aside, letting Toby absorb his new surroundings.

Eyes wide, Toby looked from the fantastic bed to the equally fantastic climbing wall, then at everything in between. Without speaking he stepped farther inside, running his hand over the new desk, then the bed. Finally, he took in the lettered art board Emma and Seth had made together, one that spelled out Toby's name. Blinking, he turned back to them. "Is this *really* my room?"

Seth reached for Emma's hand, squeezing it tightly. "Yes, it's yours."

"Wow." The word was quiet, not jubilant, and it was clear Toby was fighting tears. It was equally clear they weren't tears of sadness.

Seth walked to the closet that he had custom-built with drawers and shelves especially for Toby. He set the suitcase on the floor. "We can put your things away after dinner."

"I hope you like corn dogs," Emma said. "And French fries."

"Yeah, sure," Toby replied, still sizing up the room in disbelief.

Seth flicked on the light in the bathroom just outside the bedroom. "Why don't you get washed up?"

"Okay."

Seth and Emma retreated to the kitchen, giving Toby a few minutes to himself.

"Did you see his face?" Seth asked, his voice low.

"I imagine it was a bit like going to Disneyland and being told it was your new home."

Seth's face cleared a fraction. "Disneyland might be stretching it."

"Well, you know what I mean."

He finally smiled. "Yeah, I do." He reached for her hand. "Emma, I couldn't have done this without you. Do you have any idea how special you are?"

She guessed the lump forming in her throat equaled Toby's. "Seth—"

"Is it okay if I come in here?" Toby asked quietly, hanging back a bit in the doorway.

It was so uncharacteristic of Toby that Emma wanted to swoop him into a big hug.

This time Seth knelt beside him. "This is your home now. You can go into any part of it that you want. No restrictions, no asking permission."

Toby cocked his head to one side. "I used to get in trouble for doing that at home. My mom didn't like it."

"Everybody likes doing things in a different way," Seth explained. "I don't mind you popping in on me, champ." He put a strong hand on the boy's small shoulders. "There'll be rules, but we won't worry about them tonight. Deal?"

Finally Toby's face registered relief. "Deal."

Emma turned back to the corn dogs, near tears again. Oh, this wouldn't do. Her job was to help ease the situation, not turn it into a weepy one.

Seth showed Toby where the newly purchased dinnerware was stored and together they laid out the place settings. The stoneware dishes weren't fancy. Emma had chosen something suitable for an all-male household.

Remaining quiet, Toby ate his corn dogs and fries. Watching him, Emma could see that the excitement, fear and shock of the day had worn him out.

"How 'bout if we help put away your clothes?" Emma asked him. "Then you can get ready for bed."

"Okay," Toby agreed. No protest to stay up later.

Worry flickered in Seth's eyes and she sent him a reassuring smile. "We could all do it together."

Toby still seemed uncertain as he put away his small collection of clothing, then stowed his toothbrush in the bathroom.

"Why not get changed into your jammies, wash your face and brush your teeth? Then Seth and I can come tuck you in."

"I don't have to be tucked in," Toby replied, rolling his eyes.

"Humor us," Seth told him. "We'll be back in a while."

"Okay."

Seth and Emma returned to the kitchen.

"He's so scared," Emma murmured.

"Poor kid."

"Not anymore," Emma reassured him. "He found you."

Seth put his arms around her. "Lucky him. Lucky me."

Unshed tears ached in her throat. Forcing them back, Emma leaned her head against his shoulder. Seth held her quietly as they waited to tuck Toby in for the night.

When they returned to Toby's room, the overhead light still blazed and Toby sat on the edge of the bed. Emma switched on the small bedside lamp and Seth turned off the harsher light.

She remembered how when she was a child her mother would read her the Twenty-Third Psalm at bedtime. Emma used to always beg her mother to read "the Lord." Thinking how it had comforted her, Emma reached for the children's Bible she had placed on the shelf.

As Seth got Toby tucked beneath the

comforter, Emma flipped to the familiar passage, and then she began to read. The comforting words seemed to connect with young Toby. Even Seth was contemplative as he listened.

When she finished, Emma returned the Bible to the shelf. Then she reached forward, smoothing the dark hair that fell across Toby's forehead. "The bottom of the lamp stays on at night." She deliberately didn't call it a night-light, guessing he would think that sounded too babyish. "I hope that's okay."

"Sure."

"And don't forget," Seth added. "The bathroom's the first door on the right. My bedroom's the next one. If you get thirsty or…need anything, I'll be right there. Just holler."

Toby looked at him, then nodded.

Emma switched off the top portion of the lamp. "That okay?"

"Sure," Toby replied.

They were hesitant as they walked to the doorway. Seth glanced up, spotting the luminous constellation Emma had affixed to the ceiling. In the near-darkness all the individual planets and stars glowed.

"My little welcome present to Toby," she explained.

Seth took her hand. "Good night, Toby."

"Night," she echoed. "Sleep well."

"Night," he mumbled in return, already sounding sleepy.

All tuckered out, her mother would have said, Emma realized, missing her family. She looked down at her hand entwined with Seth's.

And it hit her how terribly much she would miss him.

Chapter Fifteen

Over the following week, Toby slowly warmed to his surroundings. Emma had been right. Toby needed to know it wasn't all going to be snatched away.

And Emma had been instrumental in nurturing that belief. She had a mother's touch, gentle and kind, which Toby responded to. Seth felt even more protective now toward both of them.

It amazed him that a child could be so grateful for so little. But it seemed Emma was as well. She treated the smallest things like gold trophies. Which is why he'd bought her the present.

He wanted to thank her...to convey to

her how much she had come to mean to him. One gift couldn't do all that. But it was a beginning. Searching through Rosewood's shops, he finally found the perfect thing. A turquoise and opal pendant. The turquoise matched Emma's eyes, which had decided him. The fire in the opal sealed the deal.

Having come to know Emma's schedule as well as his own, he watched for her car, gave her time to get inside, then waited until he heard the dogs barking in the backyard. Since Toby was now acquainted with both pups, Seth asked him to keep an eye on them while he talked to Emma.

Seth rang the bell at the front so as not to scare her.

She was obviously surprised when she greeted him. "The front door! This must be a special visit."

"Maybe."

She smiled as he walked into the living room. "You're being mysterious."

"No. Just awkward." He reached into his pocket, withdrawing the small jeweler's box. "I want you to have this."

Her hand shook a bit as she opened the lid. "Oh," she gasped. "It's beautiful!"

"I think it matches your eyes," he told her.

"But it isn't my birthday," she protested, looking from the delicate pendant back to him.

He lifted the necklace from the cushioned box, then laid the slender gold chain on her neck, fastening it at the back. "I want to say thank you—for Toby, well, for everything."

She reached for the pendant, her slender fingers caressing the intricate filigree work. "You didn't have to do this. I wanted to help with Toby. It..." Her voice wavered. "It's made me very happy."

Relieved, he smiled, then took her hand. "Good. The other reason I waylaid you as soon as you came home is because I didn't want to give you a chance to cook anything. You told me about a fancy restaurant here in Rosewood. I got so caught up in deciding...what I should do about Toby that I almost forgot about it. Anyway, how about it? Dinner with two gentlemen?"

Her eyes glimmered and he waited for her to say yes.

She glanced down at their hands. "I'm afraid I can't."

The disappointment hit him like a fist. "You already have plans?"

She blinked rapidly, glancing away quickly. "Yes."

Seth knew he hadn't spoken for her, hadn't asked her not to see anyone else, but he felt sucker-punched. He didn't know there was a competitor for her affection. "A night with the girls?" he questioned hopefully.

She shook her head. "No. Not exactly. But you and Toby go ahead. You'll have a great time."

"In a romantic restaurant without you?"

She put her fingers over her lips and he could have sworn it was to stop them from trembling. "You're exaggerating. This is your time with Toby. He thinks any place you take him is wonderful."

Still disappointed, Seth tried to read her expression, and possibly play on her soft spot. "If you're not going, I guess we'll get tacos then go over to the school for a while."

She smiled, a small, nervous smile. "I happen to know Toby loves tacos."

That was little comfort. But he tried to

look on the bright side. He could ask her again later in the week. "So, no soft feminine guidance tonight?"

Emma shook her head and again her eyes glimmered. Then she stroked the pendant. "Thank you, Seth. It's truly lovely."

Her words should have made him feel good. But he felt a prickle of unease as he left. The door had such a final sound when she closed it.

He was overreacting. Now that Toby was adjusting, he expected something to go wrong. For once he planned to shake that attitude. He was seeing trouble where there was none.

Emma sank against the door after it was closed. Hot tears swelled in her eyes, then slid quietly down her cheeks. The deep sobs didn't hit until she reached her bedroom and sat on the edge of the bed.

She hid her face in a pillow, drowning out the wails. How had she allowed herself to become this involved...to fall in love with this man?

Because she had. She wasn't sure when. Sometime during the shared pain, the compassion, she had come to know his heart.

And it was breaking hers.

From outside in the yard, she heard Toby calling to her dogs. Sundance and Butch barked happily. The dogs loved Toby's endless energy, the way he ran and played with them.

Unable to resist, she dropped the pillow and crossed over to the window. She pulled back the lace curtain and watched them. Toby had found the tennis balls she kept for them and tossed two at a time, making the dogs jump in the air to catch them. Toby's wide smile was relaxed, happy.

As she watched, Seth entered the backyard. The tall man and short child looked perfectly matched when they walked away and into his house.

She gently touched her pendant, realizing how important their safety was to her. They could never know how much she would miss them, how cutting them from her life would be a near-physical wound. She would never forget them.

Within weeks, Seth had completed the interior of the shop's new addition. The dressing rooms relocated, he then opened the alcove. He was pleased to uncover the fireplace he had been so sure he would find. Emma was right, it would be a fantastic focal point once it was restored.

He subcontracted the glasswork to the local window shop. Working with the owner, Seth had been able to design exactly what he wanted and the company manufactured new wood-frame windows, also agreeing to install them.

The old display windows were replaced with Victorian-style bay windows true to the period. They opened up the space and restored another bit of the building to its roots. Once the furnace was sectioned off, Emma's office space would be fairly easy to construct.

Seth was more than pleased with the progress. He was less pleased about his progress with Emma. For some reason he couldn't fathom, she was withdrawing.

He knew it wasn't because of Toby. Clearly she adored the boy. But after that initial adjustment period she started separating herself from them.

Seth believed her excuses. Most of them. He knew she had a huge workload, that the costumes didn't design or sew themselves. But it was more. The only time she had come back to the high school was for costume fittings. And she hadn't attended another softball practice.

Working in her shop, it would seem she would have to see Seth, but Emma somehow managed to avoid him. She'd taken on more and more outside calls for window displays even though she and Tina were buried in work.

Emma had begun sewing costumes at home rather than at the shop most days. She said it was because she could spread out more there, which was plausible considering the remodeling. But he didn't think it was the truth.

When she thought he wasn't watching, he saw the sorrow in her eyes. He'd tried to ask her about it, but she'd made an excuse and fled. And now he was afraid of pushing her farther away. Especially since he believed her behavior must be tied to her secret fear.

Deciding Tina might know something Seth approached her. "Do you have a minute?"

She smiled. "Sure. What's up?"

"Well, I don't exactly know." For the briefest moment, he wished he had Emma's talent of blurting out everything in a matter of seconds. "It's about Emma."

"Oh?" Her tone was noncommittal.

"Yeah. Do you know if anything's bothering her?"

"I don't think so." Tina studied him. "Why?"

"She isn't acting like herself."

Tina hesitated. "I have noticed that she's been twitchy lately. I figured it was the remodeling. Not that you aren't doing a great job, but it's stressful. I mean with everything being in a new place all the time. And we've got a truckload of costumes due soon."

"Yeah, you're probably right."

Tina looked concerned. "You don't think it's something else, do you?"

Clearly Emma hadn't taken Tina into her confidence. It was a telling omission. "No. Just wanted to make sure my remodeling wasn't getting too much in the way."

Tina smiled. "I *do* know Emma loves what you've done with the shop."

He managed a smile. "Good to hear."

But not what he needed to know. That would have to come from Emma. And right now he had no idea how that was going to happen.

The backyard gate stood open and her yard was empty. Emma sighed. She knew exactly where the dogs were. Like the Pied Piper, Toby was able to lead them anywhere he went.

Better they followed him home than for him to play in her yard. A twitch between her shoulder blades had caused her to watch every shadow now for a week. It wasn't anything she could put her finger on, just a premonition.

"Get it, Butch!" Toby hollered.

Toby had looked up the terrier breeds on his computer, and since then was determined to teach each of them new skills. Emma suspected he would have an early lesson on the frustration of inattentive little ones. But so far, Toby had been surprisingly patient.

"Hey, Emma!" he called out.

"Hey, yourself. How are your students doing?"

"Better. Sundance likes it 'cause at the end he gets to go through the tunnel. He likes doing that even better than digging."

"That's great." The tunnel was a plastic one Seth and Toby had rigged up.

"Guess what Seth's going to build?"

If Toby wanted it, she guessed Seth would build a space rocket. "What?"

"A fort! Like a real one, not just some old cardboard stuff. We could use it for a club-house, too. You want to be in my club?"

Touched, she tried not to give away yet another part of her heart. "I'm afraid I'm too old, sweetie. But thank you."

"Seth's gonna be in it. Are you older than Seth?"

"Of course she isn't," Seth said from the other side of the yard.

Emma hadn't known he was sitting in the dark circle beneath the trees. Flushing, she wished she'd had some warning.

"Besides," Seth added, standing so that he was visible. "It's not polite to ask ladies about their age."

"How come? Ladies always ask me how old I am."

He chuckled. "It's one of those mysteries of life that we as gentlemen simply accept."

Toby groaned. "Grown-up junk."

As he turned back to the dogs, Seth quickly crossed the yard. "Won't you join us, Emma?"

Twilight slanted over her face just enough to expose her sad smile. "I'm afraid I can't."

His voice was quiet. "You can't or you're afraid?"

Her head jerked up sharply. "I don't know what you mean."

Before she could object, he reached for her hands. "You can tell me, Emma. Whatever it is. You can trust me."

"You're imagining things." She pulled back, thrusting her hands into her pockets.

"Did I just imagine that?"

"Seth, I'm sorry if my actions implied anything more than friendship."

The unexpected blow hit him hard. "Are you saying you don't have feelings for me, Emma?"

In the shifting light he might have imagined the sudden glimmer in her eyes, the barely perceptible trembling of her lips. "Seth. I really have to go inside now. Could you have Toby put the dogs back in the yard when they're done playing?"

He watched her walk away, almost running. Escaping again.

The tension in the shop the following weeks was affecting everyone. For the first time since opening Try It On, Emma didn't want to be there. She hated avoiding Seth, ducking from one part of the shop to another to keep from talking to him.

Chastising herself for letting it go so far, for letting her emotions get out of hand, she hated the disappointment in his face.

She'd known. From the first day. But he hadn't had the same privilege. It had been up to her to keep her secret in such a way that no one else ever got hurt again. She hadn't expected that to include emotional pain.

Emma could hear the sounds of demolition in the new office area. Seth had partitioned the furnace room and was tearing into the original walls.

Tucked away in the new addition, Emma inspected the costume for the female lead in *The King and I*. It had turned out exactly as she'd hoped. She looked forward to Adam Benson's reaction to these newest costumes. He had been impressed from their first meeting by her innovative take on many of the costumes. Since his contributions to the theater enabled her to charge market value for her work, he was in many ways her benefactor, as well.

Smoothing the glistening material of the dress, Emma realized there was a strange smell in the shop. Not seeing anything, she looked toward the main part of the shop.

Leaving the costume in the workroom, she walked to the front. No one was in the display area except Tina, who was straightening up one of the new racks.

Emma's nose twitched. The smell was familiar. One she'd…

Smoke!

Terrified, Emma looked from side to side. Nothing. Then she saw it. Smoke was coming from where Seth was working. The area that didn't have smoke alarms yet.

Fear snatched her breath away as she raced up the old staircase. "Seth!"

Desperately searching, she saw the fire. Flames were traveling over one wall toward the rafters. "Seth! Where are you? Seth!"

He came at a run, immediately seeing the fire. "Fire extinguisher! Where is it?"

She couldn't speak, paralyzed by the flames.

Gently he shook her. "Tina!" he shouted. "Where's the fire extinguisher?"

"I'll get it!" Tina yelled back. She darted over to the closest fire extinguisher.

Seth ran down the stairs, intercepting her. "Call 911."

Back upstairs he squirted foam over the tallest flames.

It wasn't a huge fire. After several minutes, Seth had it under control.

"I think it's out." He turned to Emma.

She still hadn't moved. He clasped her arms, pulling her close. "Hey, it's okay. Just a small fire caused by testing the old wiring. Good thing it happened now before I finished your office."

"You're alive," she murmured, unable to believe it was true. "You're alive."

"Of course I am. Emma?"

But she was gulping for breath that wasn't reaching her lungs. The horror was real. It was now. She started to sob.

Seth held her, gently rocking her. "Emma, what is it?"

"The fire." She closed her eyes, but the tears kept coming. "The fire."

"What about the fire?"

"It killed them. Tom, Rachel. Because of me."

"Why because of you, Emma?"

She rocked, shaking her head and moaning.

He smoothed her hair. "Tell me, Emma."

Her raw voice was something between a sob and a wail. "He was trying to kill me. And he murdered them, burned them to death. Burned my precious baby."

Seth held her close, absorbing her pain, trying to understand. When the fire truck arrived, he picked her up, cradling her in his arms as he carried her down the stairs and into the back room, closing the door to intruders.

Sitting in the window, he held her in his lap as though she were a crumpled child.

He didn't have to ask any questions. The story spilled out on its own, in horrifying detail.

He could never have guessed. It explained her cryptic reply about her husband, that she was no longer married.

How had she carried this guilt alone?

He smoothed back her hair, then wiped the tears from her cheeks. "Emma, you can't blame yourself."

"You don't understand. It *is* my fault. That's why I can't let you or Toby get close. I won't lose anyone else I…care about. You have to stay away from me, stay safe."

He would never be able to stay away from her, but she wasn't ready to hear that. Outside, he could hear heavy boots on the stairs, several voices, the blast of foam from the fire engine.

But all the sounds faded away as he held her. All he heard was the quiet, troubled breathing of the woman he loved.

Chapter Sixteen

❧

From his kitchen, Seth kept watch over Emma. Butch and Sundance seemed to sense something was wrong and were snuggled beside her in the living room. And after Toby had come home from school, he'd stayed with her, too.

She'd protested weakly, saying she would be fine at home. Emma wouldn't be fine anywhere, Seth knew, but she wasn't going to be alone.

Tina had closed the shop after they left. She'd offered to help with Emma, but Seth told her to get some rest. It had been a draining experience.

Tina might yet get some rest, but first she'd made a pot of soup and brought it over. Cindy and Grace had arrived next with enough dinner to feed them for days. Another neighbor brought homemade rolls fresh from the oven.

Seth had been swamped with offers to help repair the fire damage. But it wasn't extensive, and he had it under control. When Michael phoned, Seth did confide that he hated for Emma to see the scorched walls because the fire had upset her. He didn't confide why. Emma's secret was now his and he would protect it and her with his life.

He checked the heat under the pot. He hoped she would find Tina's soup soothing.

Toby padded into the kitchen. "Is Emma gonna be okay?" he whispered.

Emma's distress obviously worried the boy. "Yeah. She just needs a little rest."

"How come she keeps crying?"

Seth knelt beside him. "Because the fire made her sad."

"But you said it didn't burn up her store."

"It makes her think of something a long time ago that was sad. She needs our help so that she can start thinking about happier things."

Toby wrinkled his forehead. "Okay."

He padded back out of the kitchen.

Seth searched the cabinets, but didn't find anything he could use as a tray. Taking out an oversized cup and saucer, he ladled out some soup and carried it into the living room, pausing in the doorway.

"Toby, this is so sweet, but you don't have to give me your teddy bear," Emma was saying.

"He helps," Toby replied simply.

Emma hugged him close. "Thank you, sweetheart. You help, too, you know. And I'm just borrowing Teddy, okay? For today."

Seth knew the stuffed toy was the most prized of Toby's new possessions. When he tucked him in each night, Teddy was always at his side. Giving it to Emma was a selfless act, especially for someone who had so little to give.

Seth backed up a few steps, then cleared his throat. "I have some soup, Emma. And Tina says you have to eat it."

Emma glanced up at him. "I'm not hungry."

"The soup's good and hot." The day was warm as they neared summer, but Emma had been so chilled, he'd wrapped her in blankets.

"A lady made house rolls," Toby added.

Emma looked at Seth for an explanation.

"Fresh out of the oven, made them herself," he explained tactfully, putting the soup on the side table.

"Toby, why don't you have one and tell me how you like it?" she suggested.

Seth seconded the idea. Once Toby was out of the room, he sat beside her. "How're you doing?"

"I'm okay. You don't have to fuss."

"I heated the soup that Tina made. I wouldn't call that fussing."

She leaned forward. "Seth, I should go home now. I don't want to put you and Toby in any more danger. Now that you know it's even worse."

"We're where we want to be."

Her face, etched with pain, crumpled.

Seth put his arms around her. "It's all right, Emma. I don't know how you kept your secret so long. It must have been eating you up inside."

"Only since I met you."

He held her close. "I'm not going to let anything happen to you."

She pulled back. "No! Then you'll be in danger, too. I can't let that happen."

She tried to get up, but Seth held her back. "You've been dealing with this on your own long enough. I'm not going to do anything foolish, call attention to you or this house. But I am going to keep watch."

"But you don't know what to watch for," she protested in a weak voice.

"And you do?" he asked quietly.

"I told you who the D.A.'s office thought was responsible."

"But it could be someone from dozens of other cases you prosecuted as well, couldn't it?"

"It's possible, but—"

"Emma, you're not getting rid of me."

"You have to keep Toby safe!"

"I will. And you, too."

"I want to believe that, but…" She closed her eyes.

Seth simply wanted to hold her close. But her fears were real. Not goblins in the night or scares that could be worked through. There was a murderer who wanted to kill Emma.

Since Davy's death, Seth had thought nothing could scare him again. He was wrong. The thought of losing Emma terrified him. And despite his assurances, he didn't have a plan to keep her safe.

But for tonight at least, she would be under his roof and his protection.

Emma ate only a little soup. Despite her continued protests, he put her in his bedroom for the night with her dogs on each side, small, determined guards.

It took longer to get Toby to sleep, and Seth guessed he was confused by the upsetting day. He probably missed his teddy bear as well.

Back in the kitchen, Seth dimmed the light and watched Emma's house from the window. Nothing looked out of place. When he'd retrieved the dogs, he'd also grabbed Emma's robe. And later he'd gone back to make sure the house was locked up tight.

Still, he felt uneasy. Probably just his reaction to hearing about her family.

He double-checked the doors, turning the deadbolts. Glad that Emma had chosen a long, comfortable sofa for his living room, Seth stretched out. She'd even bought extra pillows and blankets, which he was now using. Emma knew what it took to make a home, a family.

Davy's death had been unfair. He tried to imagine the guilt of knowing you were the murderer's intended victim. How had she hung on to her faith?

Seth heard a noise outside the window, and got up. Opening the blinds a fraction, he saw a cat walk across the window ledge, leap down and cross to the bushes.

He couldn't hear anything else. He didn't bother with the sofa, instead selecting a chair where he could see through the slatted blinds. He hadn't expected sleep would come easily. Now he didn't expect it at all.

By morning Emma was somewhat rested, if feeling foolish. She regretted having confessed everything to Seth. Now he would be protective and that would put him directly in the path of the arsonist.

Scrunching her robe closed at the neck, she made her way into the kitchen. Seth leaned against the counter, sipping from a mug of coffee. His tousled hair and the dark stubble on his face made him that much more appealing.

To see him first thing in the morning…how wonderful it would be to start each morning with him. The moment was fleeting.

Toby skidded into the kitchen, snapping her back to reality. "Do you want me to put the guys outside?" he asked, the dogs trailing him.

"That would be great." Emma smiled for his benefit. "Be sure the gate's locked after them."

"Don't you want me to stay and watch 'em?"

She shook her head. "That's okay. You have to eat breakfast and get ready for school."

"She's right," Seth added.

The boy gave up the argument easily. "Okay."

Seth reached for bowls. "Do you want

to have breakfast with us? It's just cereal but it either crackles, jumps or turns blue."

Emma was tempted. "I think I'll pass. I need to get some things ready for work."

"You have to eat," he pointed out quietly.

Emma knew it would be easy to lean on him, accept his caring and concern. It hurt her heart that she couldn't. "I'll have some toast, promise."

She turned toward the door, but he snagged her hand, pulling her back.

His kiss was at the same time tender and strong. "I'm not going to let you run away."

Emma had thought she'd used up all her tears. But fresh ones lurked just beneath the surface. Before she could give in to them, she escaped.

She walked rapidly, but Emma knew she couldn't outrun her ghosts, old and new.

After dropping Toby at school, Seth headed directly to the costume shop. He wanted to get as much of the fire damage removed as possible. Seeing Tina's car, he guessed she'd come early for the same reason.

He climbed the stairs, then stopped abruptly. "What happened?"

Tina glanced over at him. "Michael and Flynn worked nearly all night getting everything stripped and cleaned."

Seth stared in amazement. The wrecked plaster and wiring were gone. Even the damaged two-by-fours had been sandwiched with new ones. The cement floor had been swept and washed, eliminating all traces of the fire retardant. "How…?"

"Emma and Cindy are close so I called her. I'd never seen Emma freak out like that before. I thought her best friend could help. I'm guessing Cindy told Flynn."

Who apparently had gotten together with Michael. This really was some town. Sniffing, he tried to guess the new smell overriding the smoke.

"I got here early," Tina explained. "I made my own mixture of orange peel and vanilla." She took a deep, critical breath. "I have a lemon simmer potpourri going downstairs. What do you think?"

"I think Emma's going to be relieved."

"How'd she do last night?"

"She had a rough time," he replied honestly. He saw the worry on Tina's face. "The only thing she'd eat was your soup."

Tina smiled. "My grandmother's recipe. She always said it could cure everything from runny noses to premature labor."

"Soup and friendship, pretty potent combination."

Tina dug the toes of her bright red shoes against the concrete floor. "Yeah. That goes both ways. Emma's a great friend. She's never made me feel like I work for her. She's insisted that we work together, associates. That doesn't happen very often in the retail business."

"She's unique," he agreed.

"And she's here!" Tina announced, looking out the front window. "Why don't we get back downstairs so it doesn't look like we're examining the scene of the crime." The words barely out, she skipped down the old wooden stairs.

Seth followed. For the first time he noticed the pervasive odor of the lemons Tina mentioned. That and the smell of strong, fresh-brewed coffee.

Through the glass front door, Seth could see Emma's face, filled with trepidation.

"Morning, boss," Tina greeted her. "Coffee's on."

"Tina." Emma walked a little farther into the store, her pace still hesitant.

"Hey," Seth said quietly, not wanted to startle her.

Still, she looked surprised. "You're here early."

"Yes. Did you eat your toast?"

Emma blushed. "I will."

He reached for her heavy tote bag. "You want this in the workroom?"

"Well, yes, but I can carry it."

"Take Tina up on her offer. The coffee smells great."

Perplexed, Emma stayed in place as he walked away. Glancing back he could see her eyes following him.

He put her tote next to the design table and returned to take her hand. "Let's get it over with."

She didn't pretend to misunderstand, nodding in agreement.

They walked up the stairs.

As soon as Emma saw the now-clean area, she gasped. "What…I don't under-stand. Did you…?"

"The power of friends." And most likely another power, too. One he'd lost touch with. "Michael and Flynn worked late into the night."

Her face went white. "You didn't tell them?"

"Of course not. They heard you were upset by the fire. So they cleaned up the mess, hoping it would make you feel better."

Blinking rapidly, she squeezed his hand. Hard. "This is ridiculous. I never cry and now I can't stop."

"It's supposed to be cathartic."

With her free hand she wiped away her tears. "If getting all blotchy and ugly can be cathartic."

He turned toward her, gently tucking her hair behind one ear. "Ugly? Never. Inside or out."

"Seth…"

"Don't say anything. Just let me tell you this. I'd given up on life, my faith, everything. Then I met you. You started giving me hope before I had any clue how much you'd been hurt. And now knowing that—" he paused, clearing the sudden huskiness from his throat "—I realize you are my hope."

Emma pressed her face against his shoulder and he felt the heat of her tears. "If only…"

"We'll make it happen."

She pulled away, shaking her head. "No! You have to promise not to."

His heart opened even wider. "That's one promise I can't make."

Emma's lips trembled.

"No. I'll leave if I have to. I won't lose anyone else I love."

Her eyes told him she meant it. She would disappear. And as she was part of the witness protection program, it was likely he would never find her.

Chapter Seventeen

❧

The next few weeks passed in an uneasy truce. Emma plunged herself into work. The costumes for *The King and I* as well as for *Hello, Dolly!* were almost done. She only had some minor adjustments left.

Adam Benson had asked to preview the costumes. Emma could have used the time to finish the last details, but she didn't want to refuse, knowing his support kept the local group going.

For the most part, the people in the theater were locals. Benson had imported a producer and a director from L.A. to consult. He'd provided advanced training in lighting and sound for the local crew. Set design was handled much the same way.

Professionals had trained the locals and Benson commissioned the actual designs they worked on.

The community was excited by the chance to learn and everybody was proud to be putting on highquality shows. The Hill Country had become a popular retirement venue for upper-middle-class and wealthy executives and entrepreneurs, and many were drawn to Rosewood's theater. Ticket sales had remained consistent since Benson's infusion of cash.

Any other time, Emma would be excited about the beginning of another new production. It was the first time the theater was performing *Hello, Dolly!,* and she'd loved creating the lush period costumes.

Next up was *Arsenic and Old Lace,* set in the 1940s, her all-time favorite fashion era. But she hadn't given much thought to it. Her mind was too full.

"Miss Emma," Adam Benson greeted her. He was undeniably charming. It could be easy to envy a man with so much money and power. But he was remarkably likeable as well as generous. In addition to the theater, he also gave generously to the church and medical center.

"Mr. Benson."

"You've done it again. The costumes are stunning. You've got the touch, Miss Emma."

She tried to look pleased. "You're always too kind."

His wise eyes narrowed. "Something bothering you?"

She forced a smile. "Of course not. It's a joy to work with fine fabrics. Thank you for making that possible."

"I believe in supporting the community." He hesitated. "If there's anything you need, you know I'm happy to help out. Is your shop doing okay? If there's some trouble—"

"No!" Embarrassed that her feelings were so obvious, Emma did her best to look as though everything was all right. "I mean, everything's fine, but I do appreciate your thoughtfulness."

"Mr. Benson!" His assistant, Marge, called him from the stage. "I think we're ready."

"Come along, Miss Emma." He touched her elbow, guiding her up the side steps to the stage.

A photographer was on hand to take cast pictures. Immediately she glanced down the row of actors, making sure their costumes were in order. Satisfied, she turned back to Benson. "They look fine to me."

"Me, too. Now, let's put you between Roger and Elizabeth."

"Me?"

"Yes. You're the designer. I want you in my scrapbook as well."

She pushed at her hair. "I'm not really prepared."

"Can't tell that by looking," he replied, ever the Southern gentleman.

Not wanting to make a fuss, she took her place between the two actors as a series of shots were taken. Blinded by the flashes, she couldn't be sure whether there was a video camera taking footage, as well.

Eventually the session wound down. Emma helped the costume manager bag and hang the clothing. She separated the few that needed slight alterations to complete them at home.

Unlocking the front door she waited for the barrage of paws and doggie kisses. When that didn't happen, she swallowed nervously. Maybe they were asleep. But they never slept through her arrival.

She tried to listen over the sudden beating of her heart. Nothing. Afraid to walk any farther into the house, she froze.

Her glance darted over the living room as she tightened her fist around her keys. Nothing looked disturbed. She considered backing out of the front door, but what if the dogs needed her?

Fighting her fear, she crossed the room, then entered the kitchen. Still nothing. She looked through the window into the backyard and released her breath.

The dogs were playing with Toby. Carefree, he tossed balls, which they happily retrieved. She slumped against the counter, drained.

When she regained her composure, she walked outside. "Toby?" As soon as she spoke, the dogs rushed to her, demanding attention.

"Hey, Emma! Did you see how good Butch can catch no matter where I throw the ball?"

"Yes. He's doing really well. Um, Toby, how did the dogs get out?"

"I let 'em out. They were tired of being in the house."

She counted to three. "And how did you get in the house?"

"With the key. The one that says Emma."

She remembered the key Seth had insisted on in case he thought there was trouble at her house. "Does Seth know you took it?"

Toby bit his lip. "Not exactly."

"Sweetie, the key is just for emergencies."

His eyes grew serious. "Oh."

"It's all right. Just remember next time—only for emergencies. And playing with the dogs doesn't count."

"Okay."

She hesitated, but knew she had to continue. "You know you're supposed to play in your backyard, right?"

Crestfallen, he stared at her. "Don't you *want* to see me?"

Her heart splintering, Emma scooped him into a hug. "Of course I want to see you." She smoothed back the hair on his forehead. "But it's not safe for you to play over here."

"How come?"

Indeed. "Because you're alone."

"Uh-uh," he protested. "Sunny and Butch are with me."

She found it difficult to resist his logic, more difficult to resist him. "Yes, but Seth can't see you over here. What if you fell, got hurt? No one except the dogs would know. And they're good at almost everything, but they couldn't tell Seth what was wrong."

He didn't look convinced. "Then can they play in my yard?"

It simply wasn't in her to say no. "Sure. Just make sure to lock the gate when you put them back in the yard."

"Okay."

He called the dogs and they happily followed him next door.

Emma watched, the decision she'd been worrying over finally made. She had to move. Every day she delayed she was inviting trouble.

Tina could take over the shop. She ran it as much as Emma did. They could work out an arrangement if Tina wanted to buy the store, not at a profit, just for what Emma owed the bank. She wouldn't need that much to start again. At first the witness protection program would find her new housing. And after her house sold, she could use the money either for another house or business.

Head down, Emma walked back into the house. She tried to be practical. Seth could still use more furniture—that would take care of most of her things. Since her home in L.A. had burned, she hadn't collected anything else personal.

Her fingers strayed to the turquoise and opal pendant. Except for Seth's gift.

He would be hurt. But he would meet someone else, someone who could mother Toby, make them a family. Emma didn't realize she was crying until the tears splashed on her hand.

Releasing the pendant, she pushed back the curtain, watching as Seth joined Toby. He picked up the young boy, swinging him high over his head. She could hear Toby's squeals of delight. They were so good together, truly one of heaven's best matches.

She placed her hand against the window, fingers splayed across the glass. They would be part of her memories, always. Saying goodbye wouldn't come without tears.

Seth had nearly finished Emma's shop. After the electrician had rewired it, Seth attended to the final details. The dressing rooms, new racks and offices were done. Emma's office and workroom hadn't taken long as they were simple, basic rooms without built-ins. She wanted to keep the areas flexible, able to change along with her work if necessary.

He was trimming out the alcove at the front of the shop, restoring the fireplace to its former elegance. The window contractor had done a superb job. The beveled glass and wood frames looked as though they were original to the building.

Seth was satisfied with the progress. Unsatisfied with Emma's behavior. He knew she had been distancing herself and he understood why. He also knew it would take time for her to believe that was unnecessary. But she didn't seem herself at all. She was unfailingly polite, but something had changed. Something she refused to discuss.

Taking a break for lunch, he ambled down Main Street. The street hadn't changed since he'd first arrived, but now he knew its odd quirks, its welcoming details. Emma had been right about that. The town had embraced him.

Looking skyward past the trees that lined Main Street, he saw a patch of blue interrupted by only a couple of clouds. The Lord had embraced him. He had given him Toby and Emma to love.

Avoiding an approaching pedestrian, he nearly collided with one of the newspaper vending machines in front of the drugstore.

Seth barely gave it a glance when he suddenly realized what he'd seen. Digging two quarters out of his pocket, he shoved them into the machine holding the *Rosewood Digest*. Pulling out a paper, he stared at the front page. It was a picture of Emma along with two of the actors.

His stomach sank. Would it push her over the edge, make her bolt?

He walked rapidly to his truck and drove home. Emma's car wasn't parked in the driveway. Sure that no one was watching, he loped across the yard. Her copy of the local paper was tucked in the holder beneath her mailbox. He grabbed it, then, back at home, he stuffed it deep in his garbage can. Swiping her paper wouldn't buy him much time, but perhaps enough. As least he prayed it would be enough.

Chapter Eighteen

Emma picked up the telephone, dropping the receiver before she could dial. She couldn't put it off, she had to call the U.S. Marshal. But, once she told him her identity had been compromised, he would move her immediately.

And she hadn't heard back from the bank yet about Tina taking over the note on her loan. It was dicey trying to decide who to talk to first, the Marshal, Tina, the bank. Her head felt as though it was about to burst under the strain. She'd finally decided to talk to the bank first, to make sure Tina could keep the shop. Then, as soon as she'd spoken to Tina, she would call the Marshal's office.

No more putting it off, finding excuses.

Sitting at her desk in her new work space, Emma could see the shop below. It had been Seth's idea to incorporate the high, wide windows. She had privacy, but she could also survey her little domain.

And a pretty little domain it was. Seth had done a wonderful job designing the changes, then bringing them to life. The customers loved the fireplace and new alcove. People lingered over their tea and shortbread cookies. And the "purse-holders" were able to lose themselves in the generous collection of men's magazines. Seth had been right about that, too.

As she watched, Tina chattered comfortably with the only client in the shop. The pace wasn't as frantic as it had been. The pressure had been relieved with the completion of the last costumes and with the expanded and improved work space.

Glancing down at her sketch pad, Emma felt the irony of this newest job, what would surely be her last commission.

A young woman, a fan of Emma's

work, had asked her to design her bridal gown and the dresses for her wedding party. She'd tried to guide the young woman in Tina's direction, but the girl was insistent. Her expression filled with joy, she had begged Emma to understand, to help her create the wedding of her dreams.

Reluctantly Emma had agreed. If she had to leave after the design was completed, Tina could finalize details and sew the gown.

Still, Emma found her hand moving slowly as she sketched.

It would be a joy to watch these young people wed, but that wasn't possible. The dress took shape as she drew and shaded. It was a classic design, not trendy, yet not dated. A dress the young woman could eventually pass down to her own daughter. It was amazing, she realized, pausing to study what she'd drawn. A legacy to pass down through the generations.

Without volition, Emma's hand strayed to her pendant. It was a treasure worthy of such a legacy. Rachel would have grown into a beautiful woman, she was sure of it. Even at two, she'd had dark glossy hair and clear blue eyes. The most beautiful baby ever born. Certainly the most loved.

She had few pictures of Rachel. The program had discouraged her from bringing any personal photos that could betray her identity. All of Emma's pictures in her former house had been destroyed in the fire. She'd had a few photos in her office that her boss had smuggled to her. One was of her husband, another of her baby, the last was a shot of the three of them, happy.

Emma kept the photos in her bedroom; theirs were the last faces she saw each night before she fell asleep. Rachel and Tom were often in her dreams, but they weren't good dreams. Her apologies tormented her until she woke up and realized Tom and Rachel would never hear her again.

It wasn't fair that she had survived. Why had He let her live instead of Rachel and Tom? And why had He allowed her to know Seth, to fall in love with him and Toby?

She wanted only their happiness, but in her dark moments, she couldn't bear to picture them with someone else. Some other woman.

Dropping her face into her hands, she no longer saw the design on the drafting table. She saw Seth's face. She knew he would invade her dreams now, too. Especially since she wouldn't be able to say goodbye.

Randy Carter scanned the headlines of the *Los Angeles Times* spread out on the café counter. Not willing to waste his own money on a copy, he'd pulled together the sections the last customer had left. The waitress interrupted long enough to take his order and fill a stoneware mug with strong coffee.

Randy turned back to his paper, by-passing the global news. Like he cared.

Searching for the racing form, he grabbed the Arts section by mistake. Disgusted, he tossed it back on the counter; a photo caught his attention. It couldn't be.

That woman. Emily Perry.

Although the article called her Emma Duvere and she'd changed her hair, there was no mistake. He wouldn't forget that face, what she'd done to Ken.

He read the text.

Oil Baron and Philanthropist Adam Benson and Designer Emma Duvere. Small-town Dreams, Big-city Theater.

The article went on to say that the well-known Benson was a celebrity in and out of Texas, which explained why the piece had been picked up by the *Times*.

Rosewood, Texas. She'd run a long way from L.A.

The article gave a complimentary account of her costume shop, its success and reputation. Sounded like a fairy tale.

She was raking in the dough while Ken was behind bars. She'd forgotten all about him or she wouldn't have let her picture run in a paper. Thought she was safe.

She'd thought wrong.

And this time he wouldn't screw it up. He'd make sure everyone in her house was dead. And he was going to savor each moment.

A few days later, work done early, Seth waited outside the elementary school for

Toby. Cindy had been great about taking Toby home with her kids on the days Seth worked late. But he'd called, letting her know he could pick Toby up today.

He watched the tide of children pour from the school, getting into waiting cars, SUVs and minivans. From kindergarteners to sixth-graders, they all seemed to be excited, talking. The front part of the parking lot was lined with buses, which some of the kids boarded. Others hit the sidewalks to head home.

Patiently, Seth watched the kids, unable to resist picking out the ones he guessed were the same age Davy would have been.

The stream of children thinned to a trickle. He checked his watch. What was keeping Toby? He'd had to do some makeup work when he came to live with Seth because he'd been behind in his class. But he was doing a lot better now and shouldn't have been kept late by his teacher.

As Seth watched, the school buses pulled out of the parking lot one at a time. He knew the drivers waited until all the children were aboard.

He'd better go find Toby. Seth grabbed a notebook from the backseat and scribbled a note in case they missed each other.

First he walked to Toby's classroom. It was empty.

Where could Toby have gotten to?

Probably the playground, he guessed. It was the only lure Seth could think of in the school. As he walked through the nearly empty building, he saw only the janitor and a few teachers lingering in their classrooms. He didn't see Toby's teacher anywhere.

Crossing the length of the school, he pushed open the rear doors that led to the playground and scanned the swing sets and slides. No kids.

His stomach knotted as he walked farther outside. This couldn't be happening.

Then he spotted them. Toby and two other kids on the far edge of the playground. He started to call Toby's name when he realized they were fighting. He broke into a run.

As he neared them, Seth could see that Toby was fighting both other boys, giving as good as he got.

"That's enough!" he shouted.

They ignored him.

Reaching the kids, Seth pulled them apart, separating the pugilists. All three were panting and Toby tried to lunge toward one of the others when Seth released him. Grabbing his shoulder, he dragged him back. "I said that's enough. All right, what happened here?"

Sullenly Toby stared at the ground, refusing to talk.

"He started it!" one of the other boys accused.

Toby tried to lunge again, but Seth had him in a secure grip.

"Toby?"

He still didn't answer. Seth took in all three boys. He didn't know who was telling the truth, but if Toby remained quiet, it would be difficult to figure out. "What are your names?"

Startled, the two looked at each other.

"Names," Seth repeated. "Now."

"Chris Matthews," one mumbled.

"Larry Rice."

"Chris and Larry, I'm calling your parents. Now go home."

They took off at a run, not looking back.

Toby was silent as they walked to the car and drove away.

"You want to tell me about it?"

Toby looked down at his torn jeans.

"You can tell me anything, Toby."

Seth turned onto the street above the neighborhood park. Glancing over he saw two fat teardrops roll down Toby's face. He pulled the car over and parked. Turning off the engine, he got out and crossed to open Toby's door. "Come on."

Reluctantly Toby got out.

Draping his arm around Toby's shoulders, Seth led him to a secluded table in a shaded area. It was too soon for evening picnickers to be out, and the park was deserted.

Seth sat on the edge of a redwood bench and faced the boy. "What happened?"

Toby tried to fight his tears. "They said you were going to get rid of me, too."

"Get rid of you?" Seth felt Toby's heartache like his own. He pulled him into a hug. "You know that's not true."

Toby's eyes said he did think it was true.

Seth brushed away his tears. "I was going to wait a while to have this talk, but I guess now's a good time. Are you happy living with me, Toby?"

The boy nodded.

"Good. Because I'm happy living with you. So happy I want you to be my little boy."

Toby stared at him. "For how long?"

"Forever, Toby. We're a family now. I want to keep it that way."

Toby searched his eyes. "Really?"

"Really. What do you think? Would you like me to be your family?"

Toby's lips wobbled. "You mean like be my dad?"

"Yes, be your dad."

"But you'll get tired of me."

"No. You might get tired of me, though. But once you say yes, you're stuck with me. No going back."

"People always give me away."

Seth cleared his throat. "I don't."

Toby studied him. Just when Seth thought he'd come up with another question, Toby threw his arms around Seth's neck, holding on fiercely.

As he held his new son, Seth silently thanked the Lord for giving him Toby to love.

Chapter Nineteen

Emma pulled into her driveway. The day had seemed incredibly long. She'd waited in her office hoping to hear something from the bank. Still no answer. She couldn't wait much longer.

Reaching into her mailbox, she grabbed the letters and circulars. She unlocked the door, sorting the mail, wondering how much of it had to be dealt with soon.

She dropped her purse, keys and the mail on the hall table, deciding it could wait. At the same time, she realized that the dogs weren't there waiting for her.

"Toby," she muttered. She wasn't annoyed, but fear fueled her concern. He had to learn he couldn't come over here. Apparently he hadn't taken her instructions to heart.

Walking into the kitchen, she saw Butch's favorite toy on the floor. She bent down to pick it up. Funny. He always hid that one from Sundance.

Standing, she reached for the key in the deadbolt when she felt the blow to her head.

Sudden pain.

Then nothing.

Randy dragged her limp body into the hallway, the only windowless room. Walking into Emma's bedroom, he stared at her family photos. The allAmerican cozy trio. He enjoyed the sound of glass shattering as the frames hit the wooden floor.

Nothing else in her bedroom held any interest. Whiny-faced woman. She had everything. He and Ken had never had a chance, no doting parents, no education. But she didn't care. For her it was all about *the lesson*.

He could hear the dogs whining in the

closet. Stupid mutts. He'd have clocked them first, but there was a sweet satisfaction in knowing her pets would burn alive, too. Pedigreed like she was.

Self-loathing, he heaved a lamp across the room, smashing it against the fireplace. People like her had made him what he was. They took the top layer of everything and left the garbage for the rats.

He rubbed at the pain building behind his forehead. Exhausted by the drive, he wanted this to be over.

Done.

For Ken.

Seth looked out his kitchen window. He knew Emma's movements by heart. She came home, she let the dogs out in the back. Never varied.

He checked his watch. She'd been home for fifteen minutes. And the dogs weren't in her backyard. His backyard was empty, too.

Walking upstairs, he looked in on Toby. Seth decided to let him nap. After the emotional afternoon, he'd fallen asleep in exhaustion.

Deep in thought, Seth walked back downstairs. Looking out the window again, he still didn't see the dogs. In the same moment, the hair on his neck stood on end, a prickling uneasiness gripping him.

Not waiting to analyze the feeling, he whipped open the back door, taking the shortcut to Emma's. As he reached the corner of the house, he saw a man slipping out her back door, surreptitiously pulling a key from the lock.

"Hey, what are you doing?"

Carter spun around, his face mottled in anger. "What's it to you?"

Everything. "I asked what you're doing."

Carter closed the distance between them. "Repairman."

"Why didn't you say that the first time?"

Carter's fist shot out, fast, accurate. Then he ran.

Despite the blow, Seth was right behind him. Gaining on him. Seth grabbed the man, pulling him around.

Carter didn't duck when Seth punched him. Dazed, he staggered backward.

Seth pushed with all his strength, shoving Carter into the dog run. As quickly, he slipped the bolt in place and secured the lock.

"You can't stop it!" Sneering, Carter held up Emma's door key, then threw it between the openings of the wire enclosure into the deep beds of ivy and periwinkle behind him.

Terror filled Seth as ran back to his house for Emma's emergency key.

"Toby, wake up!" he shouted. "Call 911!"

Grabbing the key to Emma's house, he ran back. Trapped in the fully enclosed run, Carter was still screaming as Seth got the door to the house open.

"Emma?" He coughed against the smoke filling the kitchen. Grabbing a towel, he covered his mouth and ran into the hall.

"Emma!" Seth felt his heart stop when he saw her lying deadly still on the hallway floor.

Quickly he picked her up, unlocked the front door and rushed outside. Clearing the porch, he raced to the edge of the yard, laying her on the soft grass.

Toby ran over to them, his eyes wide as he watched Seth check her pulse.

She was breathing. In the distance Seth could hear the shrill whine of sirens.

"Is she okay?" Toby asked.

"She will be." *She had to be.*

"Where's Sunny and Butch?"

Seth looked back at the house. Smoke bulged out of the front door, the fire's main outlet. "Stay with Emma."

Grabbing the garden hose, Seth doused the towel with water. Holding it to his face, he darted back inside. He could hardly see, but he could tell the dogs weren't in the hallway. They weren't in the living room or kitchen, either. As he rushed through the rooms he pulled open all the closet doors.

Stopping, Seth listened, hoping to hear them bark.

Nothing. Except the crackle of flames.

The dogs weren't in the second bedroom that held Emma's worktable. That left her bedroom.

He paused at the doorway. The curtains were aflame, grotesquely lighting the room. He still didn't see the dogs. Quickly he ripped open the closet door. Two still small bodies lay on the floor.

He picked them up, one under each arm, and ran for the front door. He burst outside just as the fire trucks reached the house.

Hoses were rolled out and two paramedics bent over Emma.

"Anyone else in there?" the closest fireman shouted.

"No. Everyone's out."

Other firemen started hosing huge streams of water over the house.

The first fireman looked at the limp dogs. "Bring them over to the wagon."

Seth followed, handing Butch and Sundance over to his capable hands. Then he rushed toward Emma, praying as hard as he ever had. *Please, Lord.*

She was lying so still, her face covered by an oxygen mask. An intravenous drip had been started.

The paramedics waved him back as they loaded her on a stretcher.

He was aware of cars and emergency vehicles arriving. The street was aglow with flashing lights. Seeing a police car skid to a stop, Seth looked for Toby. Again his heart lodged in his throat. Then a fireman walked forward and Seth saw the boy. Still trying to stay close to Emma as instructed, Toby looked frightened and alone.

Seth climbed over a tangle of hoses and ducked between people to reach him. Taking Toby's hand in his own, he didn't plan to release it until he knew they were all safe.

A second police car arrived and the officers rushed toward the backyard. Watching them, he wondered how they knew about Carter being in the dog run.

"I told 'em you locked a bad man in the dog cage," Toby explained. "When I called 911."

Seth squeezed his hand. "Thank you, son."

A fireman approached Seth. "You need to be checked out, too."

Seth waved him away. "I'm fine."

"Still, you'd—"

"If I need help, I can get it at the hospital," Seth replied. He wasn't going to take his eyes off Emma.

Together, he and Toby watched as

Emma was put into the ambulance. Seth wanted to ride with her, but he and Toby would be in the way, hampering the paramedics' efforts.

Instead they jumped into his SUV to follow the ambulance to the hospital. Seth stayed in the wake of the ambulance.

Once at the hospital, the paramedics whisked Emma out of sight. Seth and Toby watched as the heavy swinging doors closed behind her.

Feeling lost, Seth led Toby to the waiting area. Toby still held tightly to his hand.

Seth couldn't find the words to cheer Toby, yet he sensed Toby didn't need empty condolences. Instead they watched and waited.

No one came out to give them a progress report. But not much later Cindy arrived. After a few reassuring words, she, too, was quiet.

A breathless Grace arrived next. "I spoke to Noah. He's monitoring Emma and he'll make sure she has the very best care. He'll talk to you as soon as they know something."

Seth squeezed Toby's hand. "Thank you."

Katherine Carlson approached them quietly. "Seth, I know Emma's in good hands."

He nodded.

"Michael's at her house and he'll take care of everything there." She hesitated. "Apparently the police will want to talk to you, but they have that man… Carter?…in jail."

"Did Butch and Sunny die?" Toby asked in a quavering tone.

Seth held his breath.

Katherine smiled at Toby. "No. The firemen kept Butch and Sundance on oxygen and called a veterinarian. The doctor's keeping them at the animal clinic overnight, but it looks good."

One small miracle, Seth realized.

Now they needed another.

It seemed as though dozens of hours had passed before Noah walked through the swinging doors.

Seth stood.

"Emma's resting comfortably. The blow to her head is more serious than the smoke inhalation. We'll know more when she regains consciousness."

Seth swallowed, unwilling to believe the worst. "Can we see her?"

Noah hesitated. "She needs quiet, but yes, you can see her."

Cindy stood. "I can watch Toby."

Seth gripped Toby's hand. "We both need to see her."

Noah started to protest, but then nodded.

As Seth walked forward, flashes of Davy's hospitalization threatened to overwhelm him. The antiseptic smell, the too-white walls, men and women dressed in scrubs rushing from place to place, stretchers lined up against the walls.

Toby squeezed his hand, bringing him back to the present.

Noah spoke quietly as he led the way. "We moved Emma to ICU. She's right through here."

Emma was so still it sent needles of panic through him. Seth had expected her to be hooked up to a lot of machines, but it was difficult to see, to hear their ominous beeping sounds.

He turned to Noah. "Are the machines keeping her alive?"

"No. Her heart's strong, so are her lungs. She has brain function, but she's not conscious yet. With luck, she'll wake up soon."

Luck had been elusive for Seth. Until he'd met Emma.

Noah patted his shoulder. "I'll leave you alone for a few minutes. But not too long."

Seth walked to the edge of her bed. Emma had been through so much pain, so much loss. Was she fighting to survive? Or was she giving in?

He bent close, whispering as he gently touched her cheek. "I love you."

She didn't stir, but he willed her to live. Willed her to live for him, for Toby.

"We need you, Emma. Toby's here, too. He's safe. We'll all be safe. The police have that guy, and he won't ever be able to hurt you or…anyone you love."

Toby took a step closer to the bed. "Don't die, Emma."

Seth swallowed the lump in his throat as he held the small hand in his. They'd come so far. If Emma could only go a little farther.

He and Toby continued watching her

until Noah gently nudged them from her side, leading them to the critical unit waiting area. It was a smaller, more intimate space for relatives of the most seriously ill.

As they entered, Seth saw that even more of Emma's friends had gathered. Tina jumped up when she saw him.

"No change," he told her before she could ask.

Cindy stood as well. "Toby must be tired. He can come home with me, have dinner and a sleepover with my kids. I know they'd love to see him."

Seth glanced down into Toby's frightened eyes. "Thanks, but our family needs to be together right now."

Cindy's face was filled with worry, but she smiled. "Of course."

Their group was quiet as they waited. Cindy left for a few minutes to call her children. A short time later Katherine excused herself to set up a church prayer call for Emma.

Seth remembered waiting through Davy's procedures. Each time he'd thought Davy would get better, be all right. He hadn't really believed it when the doctor told him Davy wasn't going to make it. And even when his little body gave up, Seth had refused to accept it. He'd waited for a miracle.

Waited and waited.

The minutes turned to hours. A gentle bell announced it was time for visitors to leave. Although everyone wanted to stay, Seth suggested they go home.

"She'll enjoy the company when she's awake." He didn't miss their looks of worry.

Katherine took his hands. "The congregation's praying for her, Seth."

"Thank you." He'd heard those words before.

Cindy hugged first him and then Toby.

Grace took his hand in her scarred one. "Our hearts are with you."

Tina's feet dragged. "You sure you don't want me to stay?"

"Yeah. Someone's got to get some sleep and open the shop tomorrow."

That seemed to cheer her a bit. "Okay. But call me if you need anything. I can deliver peanut butter and jelly sandwiches at 2:00 a.m. if you want them."

Emma's friends were a testament to how very special she was. But Seth needed to be alone. Except for Toby.

Another hour passed. Intently watching for a doctor or nurse, he was surprised to see Cindy, her overloaded arms full of bags.

"I thought you'd gone home," he said, reaching for the sacks.

"I'm just popping by for a minute." She reached into one bag. "I thought you and Toby might be hungry and the vending machines here are the pits. I've got roast beef sandwiches, a couple of peanut butter and jelly, too." She produced two thermoses, setting one on the low table. "The tall one's coffee." She held up the other. "And this one's milk."

Seth passed a hand over his forehead as he realized he'd forgotten to feed Toby. "Thanks."

Cindy reached into a much larger bag, pulling out two pillows and two blankets. "The sofa in here isn't bad, but it'll be more comfortable with pillows."

Seth knew he wouldn't sleep, but Toby needed it. And Cindy's kindness was overwhelming. "I don't know what to say."

"There's nothing to say. We're friends." She handed him a card. "This has my phone number, Tina's, Grace's and Katherine's. The hospital knows how to get hold of Noah if you need him, but it doesn't hurt to have his private number. We're here when you need us." Not if, but when.

She knelt to Toby's level. "You holding up okay?"

"Yeah."

"Seth's lucky he has you." She hugged him and then stood.

She was right, Seth knew. He was very lucky to have Toby.

Toby struggled to stay awake as it grew later, but his eyelids drooped as he leaned against Seth.

Easing Toby's head onto the pillow, Seth stretched the soft blanket over him. Toby had behaved like a champ. He'd kept his head during the emergency better than many adults would have done. He'd alerted both the police and the fire department. So much for such a small child.

Seth had to wait a few more hours before they'd let him see Emma again. But there was no change.

Standing by the window in the waiting room, Seth watched as dawn lightened the sky. Emma had been unconscious for more than twelve hours. The longer she remained that way, the less her chances of recovery.

He glanced up at the utilitarian clock on the wall. Enough hours had passed that he could see Emma again.

Leaving Toby to sleep, he entered her small room. She was constantly being monitored so that the nurses could see if there was any change.

There hadn't been.

Seth sat in the lone chair next to her bedside and gently picked up her hand. "I don't blame you for being scared now. But you have to know how brave you really are. Brave enough to start a new life when yours was destroyed. I wish I had your courage." He bent his head. "But I don't. I was so scared you were going to leave...." He swallowed, his voice raspy. "I didn't know when I hid the newspaper I was putting you in more danger. If I hadn't done that, you would have seen your picture, you could have called the Marshal, gotten out before Carter hurt you." He couldn't stop the tears as they ran down his face, dropping on Emma's still hand. "It's my fault, Emma. All my fault."

As he wept, he felt her fingers tremble. Fearing his mind was playing tricks on him, he lifted his head. Emma's fingers uncurled a fraction.

"Emma!" He could barely breathe as he watched her face.

Her lips parted. "Not your fault."

Seth felt his heart stutter. "Emma?" Frightened that he might disturb one of the tubes that seemed to be keeping her connected to life, he touched her cheek.

Her eyes opened. "Toby?"

"He's fine! He's great! Don't leave me again, Emma. Please."

Noah walked quickly into the room, followed by the emergency room doctor. No doubt the nurse had seen the change on the monitors.

Seth stepped back so they could reach her.

"Emma?" Noah took her pulse. "Do you know who I am?"

Her eyes focused on him. "Noah. Grace's Noah."

"Yes." He took out something that resembled a pen but when he clicked it on, pinpoints of light appeared. He checked her eyes.

The doctors consulted and Seth felt his hope stir when Noah smiled. "Apparently you're very good for her, so I'm not going to run you out of here."

"Is she—"

"First crisis averted. We'll have to watch for swelling. But if she progresses as we think she will, she's going to be fine."

"Is it all right if she talks?"

"Yes. And it's good for her to hear you." Noah patted Seth's shoulder and left. The other doctor followed, scribbling notes on Emma's chart.

"Seth?"

He leaned close. "I'm here."

"You sure Toby's okay?"

"He's perfect. You'd have been so proud of him, Emma. He was a champ."

"You're the champ," she whispered.

Seth took her hands. "I'm so sorry, Emma. I should have listened. You wouldn't have gotten hurt if I had."

"Carter's gone?"

"Forever," he promised, determined to do whatever it took to make that come true.

"You?"

"I'm here. Forever, too."

Her eyelids closed but a ghost of a smile settled on her lips.

As she drifted off, Seth uttered a prayer of thanks.

Chapter Twenty

Emma progressed rapidly, giving Noah fits until he agreed to send her home. Her house was so badly damaged it had been boarded up. The engineer reported that it was too structurally undermined to be repaired and had to be condemned.

Although several friends offered her their homes, there was only one place Emma wanted to be. Seth fixed up his bedroom for her, taking the downstairs sofa for himself.

He had also contacted the U.S. Marshal, clearing the way for a special surprise. A day later, Emma's parents arrived in Rosewood. She hadn't seen them since her relocation and, overwhelmed, Emma cried and laughed at the same time. Seth had set up a bed so they could stay in the third bedroom, close to Emma.

It still seemed like a dream. The FBI had taken over the case because Carter's crimes straddled two states. He'd been careless this time. Carter had used an ignition device identical to the one that had burned her L.A. home, linking the crimes. He'd also left a surplus of forensic material. Being caught in the act cinched the case. The feds were preferring two charges of first-degree murder, along with two of attempted murder. Randy Carter would never come after her again.

Emma could scarcely believe she could now see her family, speak freely of her past and contemplate a future.

Her parents approved of Seth and adored Toby. Her mother, Lily, was openly spoiling Toby. Her father, John, was more subtle, but keeping up the pace.

Emma crossed to the dining room window, watching the men in her life. Her father and Seth sat at the round wrought-iron table drinking coffee. Toby was chasing Sundance and Butch in one of their many games. Both dogs had bounced back and seemed no worse for their ordeal.

"How about some coffee?" Lily asked, bringing in the coffee carafe.

"Sounds good." Sitting, she saw an envelope on the table.

"When I got Seth's call, I tried to think of what I could bring you, something you really need." Lily opened the flap and slid out a stack of paper.

Not paper, Emma realized, but pictures.

"I figured yours were destroyed," Lily said gently. "But luckily I have duplicates."

And there they were. Tom and Rachel. She traced the line of Tom's jaw, knowing she would always love him.

Then she picked up Rachel's photo. Her baby. And for the first time, she wasn't sad. She saw Rachel's innocent smile, the wonder in her eyes, and she felt the joy Rachel had brought her.

"Thank you, Mom. This is perfect."

Lily patted her hand. "I'm guessing you won't be moving back to Los Angeles, will you, dear?"

Emma saw the kind wisdom in her mother's eyes. "No."

Lily smiled as she nodded. "You've found a new family, a perfect fit."

Emma wasn't sure how much she'd dreamed and how much Seth had actually said to her in the hospital. Somewhere in the mix, she'd heard *love*.

"So, when are you going to make an honest man of Seth?"

Emma laughed. "He hasn't asked."

"He's treating you as though you're fragile china, dear."

Frowning, Emma remembered one thing she was almost certain Seth had said. That her injuries were his fault.

She had to correct that notion, whether it affected a proposal or not. She loved Seth too much to let him carry an ounce of guilt. Even if that meant letting him off the hook and possibly out of her life.

It was after dinner before Emma could be alone with Seth. Friends and neighbors were still stopping in regularly. They'd brought enough casseroles and baked goods to open a restaurant. Tina dropped by at least once a day to report on the shop. Cindy, too, was a daily visitor.

And some of the neighbors came by to sympathize about the eventual demolition of Emma's house. It was a shame to lose one of the hundred-year-old homes. But Emma knew she could never have lived there again. It hurt now when she glanced over at its charred ruins.

Seth followed her gaze. "I've been thinking. I'd like to build a house. When I moved here, I didn't much care about a house. But now…I'd like something larger with a big lot."

"Sounds nice."

"You're quiet tonight."

"Just thinking of how to broach what I need to say." He tensed, so she plunged ahead. "It's about something you said at the hospital…that it was your fault."

"If I'd shown you the newspaper, you could have gotten away before Carter arrived."

"So that I could keep running the rest of my life?" She met his eyes. "Whether you believe it or not, I'm glad he came. Now it's finally over. And before you claim that guilt—" she paused for courage "—I'm afraid it's mine. I knew I needed to relocate the day I told you who I really am, what had happened. I kept putting it off, building valid excuses in my mind for the delay. So the truth is I put your life and Toby's at risk because I didn't leave."

"But he wouldn't have found you without that picture!"

"Maybe. But as I said, that would be no favor. Now that he's locked away, I can have a real life again."

"And do you know what you want in this new life?"

More than he could ever guess. "Peace, I suppose."

Sundance and Butch barked as they ran through the open back door, Toby hot on their heels.

Seth picked up her hand, the beginnings of a smile on his lips.

"Mom? Dad?" Emma looked into the guest room. It was empty. Toby's room had been empty, as well.

"Seth? Toby?"

No answer. Even the dogs were missing. What was going on?

She searched the front of the fridge, the table and counters. No note.

They could have all gone to lunch, she supposed. Without her. And with the dogs? Not likely.

Maybe it was the day for the dogs' checkup. The vet wanted to make sure they didn't show any late-onset symptoms. She checked the card tacked on the fridge with a magnet. No, that was later in the week.

Toby could have taken them for a walk. After all it was Saturday, and he didn't have school.

The phone rang and Emma snatched up the receiver. Although always pleased to hear from Cindy, it was difficult to concentrate while they chatted.

As she hung up the phone, the doorbell rang. "Don't worry. I'll get it," she said to the empty house.

Prepared to accept another casserole or plate of cookies, she opened the door. Her mouth, however, opened of its own volition.

Seth and Toby stood on the front porch, dressed in identical navy blue suits, stiffly starched white shirts and new black leather shoes. Even Toby's small tie was a duplicate of Seth's. And they carried matching bouquets of flowers, sized to fit their disparate pairs of hands.

Seth's eyes twinkled.

But Toby was the one who spoke. "We've come to ask you something."

Swallowing her surprise, Emma tried to match her tone to Toby's serious one. "I see."

Toby looked up at Seth.

Emma did, too.

"Yes," Seth said in an equally somber tone. "We've come to ask if you'll marry us. And if you'll have us, we promise to love you the rest of our lives."

Emma's fingers flew to her mouth as ridiculous tears filled her eyes.

"Aw, you made her cry," Toby muttered.

Seth pinned him with a pointed look. "She still has to give us an answer."

"Yes!" she shouted, somehow getting past the flowers into Seth's arms. "Yes, yes, yes."

"I love you, Emma-Emily," Seth whispered.

"And I love you."

Their lips met, sealing the promise that

had begun in a display window aeons earlier.

Toby tugged on her skirt, then on Seth's sleeve. "I love her, too."

Breaking apart, they picked him up, including him in their circle of love. Flower petals from the bouquets scattered over the lawn as they whirled him around.

Emma's and Seth's lips touched again, the kiss a promise to cherish. Because now they had a new beginning, a new family and all the love they deserved. In a little town called Rosewood, where big dreams come true.

* * * * *

Dear Reader,

Wounded. A word that conjures up sympathy, empathy and pain. But to Emma Duvere and Seth McAllister, it is something that draws them together, erases barriers and sets them on a path to love. In the small town of Rosewood, Texas, the healing begins.

I believe that in any place, large or small, amidst a circle of caring friends, new life can flourish. I have been blessed with the best of friends. This is what I wish for you. Along with the hope that you will enjoy the journey of these two very special people.

God bless,

Bonnie K. Winn

And now, turn the page
for a sneak preview of
NOTE OF PERIL
by Hannah Alexander, the first title
in Steeple Hill's exciting new line,
Love Inspired Suspense!
On sale in July 2005
from Steeple Hill Books.

Chapter One

Colorful hues from multiple spotlights streaked across the stage in laser precision. The floor vibrated with the impact of drums as Grace Brennan smiled up at her *Star Notes* costar, Michael Gold.

"I saw you watching me from the corner of your eye," Michael sang, leaning forward and giving her a long, sultry look. "You like me, I can tell."

With an audacious wink at the audience, Grace placed a hand on Michael's chest and pushed him backward. "I know you think you saw something you did not see. I like my hound dog just as well."

As they continued their comedic duet,

Grace felt a familiar tingle. Michael could sizzle the bark from a tree in January with those smoldering dark eyes. And his voice was on a par with Josh Groban's.

Three vocal backups, Cassidy Ryder, Delight Swenson and Blake Montana, joined them onstage, and the *Star Notes* show breezed on with all the energy and laughter of a typical night.

The interactive show—like a country *Star Search*—had become so popular that the waiting list for guest amateur appearances was ridiculously long. The audition manager chose only the best vocalists, and the winner of each show was invited to return for further competition.

The theater was packed tonight due to the influx of tourists into Branson on the Friday after Thanksgiving. As the appreciative audience continued to applaud, Michael announced their final amateur guest vocalist of the evening. She came on stage and on cue began her ballad with the *Star Notes* performers providing backup and harmony.

The *Star Notes* cast had intense practice sessions daily, and their expertise showed.

They could make almost any voice sound good. The ongoing oneliners and repartee—which changed from night to night—kept the crowds coming back for more.

As the guest ended her song and turned to leave the stage, Grace invited another round of applause.

Michael took Grace's hand and kissed it. She met his dark gaze with a searching one of her own, and her skin tingled where his lips touched. Fresh cheers rose from the crowd.

When the *Star Notes* director, Henry Bennett, had added romantic interaction to the show's script last year, the crowds had responded with enthusiasm. So had Michael. Only Grace continued to have misgivings about it. Sometimes she couldn't help wondering how much of what went on between herself and Michael was an act, and how much was real. And lately she wondered about it after every performance.

As the applause died and the theater lights came on, Grace eagerly anticipated the final phase of the show. She loved talking with the audience.

An usher came down the aisle carrying a single bouquet of red roses and a gold foil package. He stepped onto the stage and presented the items to Grace with a flourish. "Delivery services brought these for you, Miss Brennan."

The cast of the show often received flowers, gifts and cards from fans. Gifts brought onstage during the final few moments of the show added to the "reality" ambiance—another of the director's ideas.

The card with the roses read "From your biggest fan," and it was signed, "With love, Michael."

She read the note aloud, waited for the catcalls and applause to die down, then grinned up at Michael as he took the bouquet from her arms so she could open the lid of the package.

She pulled out a music box of stained glass and caught her breath. The jeweled colors reflected the stage lights with sparkling intensity in its artistic representation of a winding, white-capped river.

"It's beautiful," she breathed, touching the box reverently. She looked up at Michael. "It's—"

But she caught him frowning at the gift, and saw the barely detectable shake of his head.

Okay, so this wasn't from him. She lifted the lid, and music from the song "The Water Is Wide" spilled across the auditorium as its notes were picked up by her microphone.

The tune chilled her with unwelcome memories.

A gold embossed card lay on the velvet lining of the interior. With carefully concealed reluctance, she pulled it out and scanned the childish scrawl on the elegant card. The chill in her spine intensified.

Cheaters never prosper. Remember the contest? Soon everyone will know. There are some things time won't erase. And this is just the beginning.

Grace froze at the accusation. The chatter seemed to fade around her, and she grew intensely aware of the waiting audience.

She forced her smile back into place. No time to think about the ominous note now, or what lay behind it. She passed the gift to Delight, the youngest and most energetic member of the cast, who always welcomed a chance for the limelight.

Snap out of it, Grace, she told herself. *There'll be time to think about this later.*

Michael frowned at the momentary look of shock in his costar's aquamarine eyes. Something was wrong. Just for a second, Grace's smile didn't quite fit.

The impression disappeared, but he studied her as she chatted with apparent spontaneity, charming her way into hearts as she always did—as she'd long ago done with him. But Grace didn't realize the effect she had on people.

For the final set, she had changed into a satin-and-lace gown the rich color of dusky purple, and had caught her hair up in a rhinestone clip. Her face glowed with healthy color. She had been discovered by Henry, the *Star Notes* director, in an amateur contest eight years ago. Henry had quickly recognized Grace's potential. Not only did she have a beautiful voice with exceptional range, but she was also a talented songwriter, whose words touched the very soul.

Michael doubted anyone else had noticed Grace's lapse of composure over the mystery gift. At last, she thanked the audience for being there, and amid renewed applause made her way from the stage. Michael followed. Henry had called a meeting in the green room after the performance. They all knew the director would be waiting for them.

"Hey, Michael, you pulling some kind of prank?" called the band's drummer, Peter, as the rest of the cast filed along the wide hallway backstage.

Michael glanced over his shoulder at the man with spiky short hair and a hole in his ear—on Henry's stage, men weren't allowed to wear earrings or other jewelry that involved body piercing. "Prank?"

"What'd you do, ask her to marry you?" Blake Montana, the lead guitarist and bass backup, nudged Peter in the ribs.

Peter snickered. "Yeah, she looked sick."

Blake laughed, and the two jokers high-fived each other as Delight rolled her eyes at their juvenile humor.

Michael pulled off his cowboy hat as he

glanced toward Grace, who walked alone several yards ahead of them. He knew she could hear the teasing, but she didn't respond or even turn around. Ordinarily she'd be bantering with the rest of them.

Michael excused himself, caught up with her and took her hand. "They think I sent the music box."

"I know you didn't," she said softly.

"So who did?" he asked.

"A secret enemy."

He glanced over his shoulder to make sure no one was listening. "I take it the card wasn't filled with good wishes."

"Definitely safe to say that."

He frowned. "Bad note?"

She nodded. "You can read it later."

"Who was it from?"

"I might tell you if I knew."